GOD HELP YOU
MERRY GENTLEMEN...

Arriving home early after spending Christmas
in jolly old England, sometimes amateur sleuth
Adrien English discovers alarming developments
at Cloak and Dagger Books—and an old
acquaintance seeking help in finding a missing
boyfriend.

Fortunately, Adrien just happens to know a
really good private eye...

SO THIS IS CHRISTMAS
The Adrien English Mysteries, Book 7
December 2017
Copyright (c) 2017 by Josh Lanyon

Cover by Johanna Ollila
Book design by Kevin Burton Smith
Edited by Keren Reed
All rights reserved

ISBN: 978-1945802027
Published in the United States of America

JustJoshin Publishing, Inc.
3053 Rancho Vista Blvd.
Suite 116
Palmdale, CA 93551
www.joshlanyon.com

This is a work of fiction. Any resemblance to persons living or dead is entirely coincidental.

TABLE OF CONTENTS

*To Jaime Wilson--
archeologist, adventurer
and all-round lovely person*

SO THIS IS CHRISTMAS

THE ADRIEN ENGLISH MYSTERIES
BOOK SEVEN

JOSH LANYON

CHAPTER ONE

"**Y**ou don't remember me, do you?"

I looked up from the latest love note sent by the California State Franchise Tax Board and offered what I hoped was a pleasant smile. Between the taxes, the jetlag, and the unwelcome discovery that my soon-to-be-demoted store-manager stepsister was using the flat above Cloak and Dagger Books as some kind of love shack, pleasant was about the most I could manage.

Medium height. Blond. Boyish. As I stared into an eerily familiar pair of green eyes, recognition washed over me. Recognition and astonishment.

"Kevin? Kevin O'Reilly?" I came around the mahogany front desk that served as my sales counter to give him a…well, probably a hail-fellow-well-met sort of hug, but Kevin didn't move. He grinned widely, nodded, and then—unexpectedly—his face twisted like he was about to burst into tears.

"Adrien English. It's really you." His voice wobbled.

"Hey," I said. I was responding to the wobble. My tone was a cross between warm and bracing. Alarmed, in other words.

Kevin recovered at once. "It's only…I figured it couldn't be the right store. Or if it was, you'd have sold the business and moved to Florida."

"Moved to Florida?" Did anybody move from Southern California to Florida? Did Kevin remember me as an elderly Jewish retiree? No.

Kevin was just talking, mouth moving while he stared at me with those forlorn eyes. Trying to make his mind up.

About what?

He looked...older, of course. Who didn't? And thinner. And tired. He looked unhappy. There was a surprising amount of that during the holidays. And even more after Christmas. Which is what this was. The day after Christmas.

Boxing Day, if we had stayed in London.

Which we hadn't.

"Wow. This really is a surprise," I said. "Is it a coincidence? Or were you actually looking for me?"

"Yes." Kevin hesitated. "No."

I laughed. "Good answer."

Kevin opened his mouth but changed his mind at the thump of footsteps pounding down the staircase to our left.

Natalie, my previously mentioned stepsis and soon-to-be-demoted store manager, appeared, looking uncharacteristically disheveled—though I've been duly informed that smudged eye makeup and "bed head" is a real thing and supposedly sexy. Angus, my other business investment mistake, was on her heels. Right on her heels. In fact, they nearly crashed down the staircase in their hurry to stop me from whatever they thought I was about to do.

"Adrien, it's not what you think!" Natalie clutched the banister as Angus lurched past her.

Why do people always say that?

I spluttered, "Seriously? *Really?* Are you kidding me, Nat?"

Angus, having avoided knocking Natalie down, promptly tripped over Tomkins, the beige alley cat I'd rescued six months earlier. The cat was apparently also fleeing my wrath, though he'd been the only innocent party at that...party.

I held my breath as Angus managed to hurdle the last three steps and deliver a barely qualifying 12.92 landing on the ground floor.

I glared at him. "And *you*. You stay out of my sight."

He shrank inside his gray hoodie like a retiring monk, which he was demonstrably not. Note to self: next time hire a headless monk.

"I'm fired?" he gulped.

Natalie gasped.

"Hell no, you're not fired. In the middle of the holidays? Wait. Maybe you are fired. I have to think about it. Meantime maybe you could bring yourself to reshelve the week's worth of books sitting on this cart?"

Angus leaped to obey.

"It's not a week's worth," Natalie said with a show of defiance. "You haven't been gone a week. That's two days' worth, and we didn't have time to reshelve because we were busy *selling* books."

"And you were busy *not* selling books. But we'll discuss it later."

"Fine. Okay. Yes, Mr. Scrooge, we did take Christmas off."

"And other things too, it seems, but like I said, we'll discuss later. Right now we have customers."

She looked at Kevin.

"Not him."

"*Where?*" she demanded, mutiny in her blue eyes. Flecks of green glitter dusted her model-like cheekbones.

Right on cue, the bells on the door chimed in silvery welcome, and I had to smother a grin at her irate expression as a pair of elderly, male professorial types wandered in, each clutching what looked ominously like bags of books for return.

"Want to grab a cup of coffee?" I asked Kevin, who had observed the last three minutes in astonished silence.

"Sure," Kevin said.

"We'll let these two get their story straight before I cross-examine them."

"Oh, so funny," Natalie muttered.

I did laugh then, although she was right. It wasn't funny, and Natalie + Angus was an unexpected and unwelcome equation both in the work place and every other place I could think of. Which is why it seemed like a good idea to step away before I said things I might regret.

Plus I desperately needed caffeine. To add to their other offenses, Natalie and Angus had pinched every last coffee bean in the building. I'd had to choose between coffee and nine more minutes with Jake that morning. Which went predictably. My gaze veered automatically to the clock on the faux fireplace mantel. Jake ought to be walking into his meeting about now. He'd headed out to meet a client as I'd left for the bookstore. We were hoping to rendezvous for lunch—and just the idea of that, of being able to casually meet Jake for lunch, instantly warmed me.

We left Natalie distractedly greeting customers, and I led the way out of the store into the damp, chilly Monday morning. The smell of last night's rain mingled with street smells. The gutters brimmed with oily water, and the street was black and slick. The fake evergreen garland and tinsel-fringed boulevard banners looked woebegone and windblown—like they'd gone to bed without taking their makeup off.

All the same, it felt weirdly festive. Like the dark side of Christmas.

"Is it always like that?" Kevin asked as we jogged across the already busy intersection.

"More or less. I prefer less." I threw him a sideways smile.

His brows drew together. "You haven't changed at all."

"Now there you're wrong."

"No, but I mean you look exactly the same. You look great."

"Thanks. It's the Wheaties." And the successful heart surgery. Being happy probably didn't hurt either. I pointed down the street at the blue and white umbrellas crowding the sidewalk in front of the indie coffeehouse, and we veered from the crosswalk and hopped the brimming gutter, just missing getting splashed—or worse—by a Mercedes who didn't notice the crosswalk *or* us.

I said, "How long has it been? Three years?"

"About. It feels like thirteen." He looked like it had been thirteen. There were shadows beneath his eyes and lines in his face even though he couldn't be much more than twenty-eight. Out of college and doing archeology for a living? Could you make a living doing archeology?

Probably as easily as you could selling books for a living.

"So how've you been?" I prodded his sudden and complete silence. "How was your holiday?"

His face twisted again. "If you'd asked me last week—"

We'd reached the coffeehouse. I held the short, wrought-iron gate for Kevin, and as we reached the glass door entrance I gave him an encouraging shoulder squeeze—*hold-that-thought!* The life-affirming fragrance of hot coffee and baked goods wafted out.

"Find us a table." I headed for the mercifully short line. "What do you want?"

"I don't care," he said. "A tall, pumpkin spice latte with caramel drizzle and no foam."

Uh-huh, as the philosophers say.

"Got it."

I placed our orders and eventually located Kevin at a tiny table behind a large potted tree festooned with red bows and white fairy lights. He had his head in his hands, which is never a good sign in someone you're planning to have coffee with.

I pulled out the chair across from him. "Something tells me this is about more than not getting a Red Ryder BB gun for Christmas. Why don't you tell me what's going on?"

The words came out muffled behind his hands. "I don't know where to start."

I sighed mentally. I'm all for extra helpings of comfort and joy this time of year, but I was more than a bit sleep deprived, and I was worried about the situation with Natalie and Angus. Still.

"Start at the beginning. What are you doing in my neck of the woods? Are you visiting family?"

"No. My family's all up north." He raised his head and took a deep breath. "I'm looking for someone."

"Who?"

"Ivor. I've checked the hospitals, the morgue. The police won't help because his family won't report him missing and he's an adult. They say he's got a right to disappear if he wants."

"I'm sorry," I interrupted. "Ivor is…?"

"Missing."

"Right. I mean, who or what is Ivor to you?"

"He's my boyfriend."

"Oh, that's great!" Possibly I sounded overly enthused, but as I recalled, Jake had not taken kindly to Kevin's, er, boyish interest in me. Or mine in him. Not that I'd ever *really* been interested in Kevin.

Anyway, it was all a long time ago.

"Yes. It was. Is. And that's why—" Kevin broke off as the barista brought our coffees and a couple of pastries on a tray.

In a mystery novel, that would have been the point at which a silencer would have appeared through the branches of the potted tree to take out Kevin, but in real life we just waited politely until she departed.

"Have some baklava," I said, "and let's walk this back a few steps. Ivor is your boyfriend, and he came down south to spend the holidays with his family, and now he's missing?"

"Yes. Right. Exactly." Kevin reached for a slice of baklava.

"And his family is saying…what?"

"Nothing."

"Meaning they won't talk to you or they don't have any information?"

Kevin chewed like a threshing machine and spit out, "Both."

"It can't be both."

"First they said he wasn't there. Then they stopped talking to me."

"Ah. So you think—"

"He didn't change his mind about us! I know he's there. Something happened while he was down here visiting them."

Yep. And that something had led Ivor to change his mind about being with Kevin. Been there and done that. And honestly, it had all turned out for the best. As painful as it had been getting dumped by Mel, I didn't regret a minute of that heartbreak because my path had ultimately led to Jake.

I didn't try to tell Kevin that, though. I didn't tell him if it was meant to be, it would happen. I didn't reassure him about all the fish in the sea. Because it doesn't help when you're in love with a particular fish.

"What do you think happened?" I asked.

"I don't know."

"Realistically, I mean."

"Realistically, I don't know. Nothing they could say would make any difference to him. I know Ivor. I know he loves me."

I have to admit his absolute certainty was convincing. Or maybe it was just poignant.

I said tentatively, because sometimes hearing it aloud jolts you back to reality, "Do you think he's being held against his will?"

"Maybe." He said it more in challenge than in belief.

"What do you think would be the purpose of that?"

"Maybe they would try to force him into conversion therapy? They're really conservative. I mean like something out of the nineties."

"Uh…" Presumably he didn't mean 1890s.

"I didn't even think normal people *could* feel that way now," he said all wide-eyed and shocked-looking. Seven years wasn't a generation, but Kevin had grown up in a different world than me. Certainly a different world than Jake.

"I'm not sure how normal they are if they're really holding their son against his will so that they can force him into conversion therapy."

"I mean normal-*seeming*. People who live in the real world. Who've been to college. Who have jobs. Friends. Who have money."

That caught my attention. "They have money?"

"A lot of money." He said it with complete disgust.

"What's Ivor's last name?" I asked.

"Arbuckle."

"*Arbuckle?* As in Candace and Benjamin Arbuckle?"

Kevin watched me, torn between hope and unease. "Right. Why? Do you know them?"

"My mother knows them. I went to school with Terrill."

I hadn't thought of Terrill in years. And I'd have been happy to go on never thinking of him.

Kevin was staring at me expectantly. I admitted, "I vaguely remember Ivor. There was a sister too, I think."

"Jacintha. Yes." Kevin continued to wait for my pronouncement.

I didn't have a pronouncement. If I did, it would be something along the lines of *Run for the hills!* Terrill and I had been doubles partners on the tennis team back in high school. He was a good player but a total prick off the court. Happily, once my health had sidelined me, I'd never had to deal with Terrill again. As in literally never. I'd never seen or heard from him again after I got sick.

Terrill Arbuckle as an in-law was something I wouldn't wish on anyone—or at least not the Terrill Arbuckle I'd known back then. And I couldn't imagine the rest of the clan was any better. That was an assumption. I didn't know it for a fact. Maybe Ivor was the white sheep of the family.

Kevin gazed beseechingly at me with those wide green eyes. He said huskily, "Do you—could you—can you help me, Adrien?"

"*Me?* Well, I don't know how much help I'd be. I do know—"

"You saved me," Kevin broke in, and he sounded startlingly passionate about it. "I'd have gone to prison for murder if you hadn't stepped in three years ago. Nobody else believed me. Only you. Well, also Melissa. Anyway, I never got the chance to tell you. Never got the chance to say thank you."

"That's okay. You didn't have to."

"When I saw your bookstore, it was like a sign. I mean, I know that probably sounds crazy, but I was driving around feeling so—so desperate and alone, and then when I saw you, I knew it would be okay. I *knew* you would help. That I'd managed to find the one person who could help."

"Okay, but wait," I said quickly. "First of all, you're welcome for three years ago. I couldn't have done that on my own, though. And really the same goes for now. I'd like to help, but probably the most helpful thing I can do is put you in touch with someone who *can* get you some answers."

"Who?" Kevin asked blankly.

I smiled. Because even in these not very cheerful circumstances, knowing I could call on Jake for help, could count on Jake now and forever, filled me with…happiness.

Yeah. Happiness.

"Jake Riordan," I answered.

CHAPTER TWO

"*Him?*" Kevin said, and he did not seem to be sharing my happiness. "*That* guy? The cop? You're kidding. Is *he* still around?"

"Yes," I said. "He's still around. He's a PI now. He's also my…" I can't explain why I felt so self-conscious saying the word. Maybe because it was still a word new to my vocabulary. Maybe it was because Kevin's tone reminded me that not everyone was overjoyed that Jake was still around. That plenty of people were just as astonished as Kevin.

"Partner," I finished.

"You're kidding," Kevin said again.

"No. I'm not kidding."

"You mean like really your partner or you're in the PI business together?"

I swallowed my exasperation. "Really my partner. Yes. We live together. I'm not in the PI business. He is."

"Wow," Kevin said. "I did not see *that*. No way."

"Yes way," I said with a hard and determined cheerfulness. "We're still together." Not counting the two years when he wasn't and we weren't.

"You're a *way* better detective than him," Kevin told me.

That made me laugh. "Not so much—though I can't wait to tell him you said so. Anyway, I'm meeting him for lunch, so I can talk it over with him then. Where are you staying?"

Kevin gave me the particulars of his hotel and then said cautiously, "Is Jake expensive? Because Ivor and I don't have a lot of money. When he came out, his family cut him off financially."

Of course! Because what Jake needed right now when he was struggling to get his business off the ground was me saddling him with another pro bono case.

"We'll figure something out," I promised. I glanced at my watch, finished my coffee, and said, "I've got to get back to the store, but I'll call you this afternoon."

"Okay." He was still gazing at me with all that hope shining in his eyes.

It weighed my heart down because I didn't think this was going to end well for Kevin.

"Try not to worry. One thing I've heard from Jake over the years is that most of the time someone goes missing, it turns out to be nothing. They show up a while later, and they're perfectly okay. The odds are, Ivor is fine. He may just need some time to think."

Kevin shook his head, not bothering to answer.

"Or maybe not. But do me a favor. Keep a low profile. Don't try to contact the family again. If they think you've given up, their guard will go down, and that would be better."

He brightened. "You know a lot about this stuff."

"Uh, no. I honestly don't. That's commonsense. So go back to your hotel, and rent a movie or something. I'll be in touch."

* * * * *

Let nothing ye dismay...

There seemed to be a lull in the stream of post holiday returns, and the bookstore was quiet and mostly empty when I pushed inside. In the background Sarah McLachlan softly reassured the merry gentlemen and anyone else who was listening, while the rain made *flick-fleck* sounds against the windows. Natalie and Angus stood in a huddle behind the tall counter—not a romantic huddle, a co-conspirator kind of huddle—but they guiltily jumped apart at the cheery warning jingle of the door.

"Angus, can you handle things for a few minutes? Natalie and I need to ta—*whaa?*"

Nothing will make you lose your train of thought faster than a cat pouncing on your head.

Tomkins, who was part-Abyssinian and part-kamikaze pilot, had developed a fondness for prowling the tops of the towering bookshelves and dropping down on me at unexpected moments, like my own personal Cato Fong.

"The hell, cat!" I clutched at my cat-hat. Tomkins gave my face a couple of friendly swats—claws in 'coz we're pals, fortunately—before I lifted him off, but clearly I was not nearly as menacing a figure staggering around trying to remove a feline limpet from my head as I'd been two seconds earlier. Natalie was smirking, while Angus turned purple, as though about to combust with the effort of not laughing openly at me.

"We are not amused," I said, although I think Tomkins was.

"You were saying?" Natalie spluttered with merriment.

I handed Tomkins off to the nearest shelf, which coincidentally carried a row of Lilian Jackson Braun's *Cat Who* books. "I was saying you and I are going to have a chat. Now."

That wiped the smirk from her face, and she followed me into the tiny back office. However, if I thought she was going down without a fight, I was sadly mistaken.

And, more sadly, not for the first time either.

No sooner had I closed the door behind us than it was launch on warning.

"You had no right to burst in on me like that this morning, Adrien! I'm not a child. I'm entitled to my personal life. I know you own the building, and you're family, but I should still have the same rights and benefits as any other tenant."

"What? *Whoa*. First of all, I didn't even know you'd be upstairs. I didn't think you were here at all. You were supposed to be at the house, taking care of Scout. It was an hour past when the store was supposed to open."

"You thought it was okay to barge in on Angus?"

"Ye-*no*! I wasn't sure what was going on. The store should have been opened, and everything was still locked up."

"Oh my God! Do you know how *late* we worked Christmas Eve?"

"No. How would I know? I said you could close early."

She pointed at me like a TV prosecutor springing her carefully laid trap on a guilty witness. "We were busy, so we stayed open until the last customer had gone at *ten o'clock on Christmas Eve*."

I noticed—belatedly, I admit—that she had colored her hair over the holiday. Natalie, like her older sister, Lauren, is a natural blonde. For some reason she had dyed her hair dark except for two thick swatches in the front, which she had bleached…white.

I couldn't seem to stop staring at those platinum tresses. Something about them struck me as ominous.

I said automatically, "Okay, well, that was really nice of you, and I appreciate it—I really do—but I didn't *ask* you to do that. I didn't want you stuck here on Christmas Eve. And it doesn't change the fact that—"

"We did it because it was the right thing to do, but then you burst in this morning and scare us to death, and all but accuse us of—"

"Wait a minute," I interrupted. "I didn't 'burst in.' I unlocked the door and walked inside. I already said I didn't know you were up there, let alone that you and Angus were— That is *not* an image I wanted in my brain, okay? I didn't realize you were staying here too."

"I wasn't! Most of the time. But since I'm going to be renting the upstairs, I thought this was a really good time to start moving my stuff in."

"Yeah, but—"

"If you've changed your mind about me staying here, say so!"

"I didn't change my mind!"

I always thought I was a pretty good debater. Then I inherited three sisters, and I learned that I was but a grasshopper flittering before the Prada-clad feet of Shaolin masters. On my best day I couldn't even snatch the pebble from fourteen-year-old Emma's hand, and right now I was getting clobbered by Natalie.

"Okay, *wait*," I said. "This is completely off the track. The subject is *not* do I want you for a tenant or will I respect your privacy once you're officially my tenant. The subject is what the hell are you doing f-boinking," and here my voice dropped to a hiss, "*Angus*."

She hissed right back, "Angus is not a child and neither am I! Since when did you turn into such a prude?"

"I'm not a prude. This isn't a judgment on your taste in men—or Angus's taste in women. My concern here is Cloak and Dagger and how this is going to affect business."

"Oh, I don't *believe* this!"

"You're technically his boss, Nat. You're the store manager."

For a split second that seemed to register with her. She recovered fast.

"Oh my God. That's a formality and you know it. *You* manage this store. You're a total control freak."

"*What?* I am not!"

"Anyway, you think Angus is going to sue me for sexual harassment? You think he's going to sue *you*?"

Nope. I thought he was going to fall in love with her, and she was going to dump him, and he'd mope around for a week and then quit, and we'd be back to Natalie and me trying to run the place on our own.

I didn't make the mistake of saying that—mostly since she didn't give me a chance.

Tears sprang to her eyes. Like on cue. Like Meryl Streep going for her twentieth Oscar nomination. "If you want me to quit, go ahead and say so." Her voice trembled under the weight of that sea-level rise.

"I don't— I didn't— I want you to stop f-fraternizing Angus."

"That's just great!" The high tide of tears welled and spilled over her cheeks. "Well, I can't put *that* genie back in the bottle."

Head held high, like a doomed princess on her way to the gallows, she swept past me and out of the office.

"What the hell just happened?" I asked the universe.

"You're talking to yourself again," the universe replied, pushing open my office door.

Okay, it was Jake, but he was kind of my universe.

For a guy who'd had less sleep than me, he looked unfairly refreshed and vital on a damp and drizzly Monday morning. He wore boots, jeans, a tailored white shirt, and a brown tweed blazer, which brought out the gold glints in his hazel eyes. His blond hair was silvering at the temples and a fraction longer than he used to wear. He was still hard and fit, but he'd lost that gaunt, haggard look he'd had six months ago when we'd met up again after two years apart.

In fact, he looked healthy and relaxed. Like he'd really spent the last few days on vacation instead of the family holiday from hell.

"*Hey*," I said, by way of greeting. I won't say I actually fell into his arms, but I was pretty happy to see him.

"Hey yourself," Jake replied and kissed me, the warm pressure of his mouth firm against my own.

Hard to say—and it was a theory I planned on testing a lot over the next forty years—but I didn't think I'd ever get tired of kissing Jake.

Even these quick perfunctory kisses—well, it had started out quick and perfunctory, but the taste of him: that weirdly erotic blend of coffee and breath mint; the smell of him: an even weirder erotic blend of suitcase and Le Male aftershave; and the warm weight of his hand on my shoulder, drawing me in close, closer...

Reluctantly, we parted lips.

"Jesus, I missed you." He smiled into my eyes.

"Same here."

"I got used to spending all day every day with you."

I said regretfully, "If only it paid better."

There was definitely a sparkle in his eyes. "Well, I might have some good news on that front. Are you ready for lunch?"

I laughed. "Lunch? It's ten thirty in the morning."

"Is it?" Jake glanced at the clock on my desk. "It feels a lot later."

"It's been a long morning," I agreed.

"Everything okay?" He took a closer look at me. "Is Natalie okay?"

"I think so. I hope so. You know what, why *don't* we get a coffee or something? I need to get out of here for a while."

True, I'd only been *in* there about five minutes. It was just like old times.

His dark brows rose. He said, "Sure. You want to walk, or you want to take a drive?"

I grabbed my black overcoat. "Let's walk."

When we stepped outside the bookstore, the rain had softened to a light, shimmering mist. More like holiday décor than actual wet.

Christmas is the only holiday I can think of where it continues to feel like holiday-in-progress even the day after. Maybe because people were still bustling around with heavy shopping bags, and the Eagles were plea-bargaining from storefront speakers.

If not for Christmas, by New Year's night...

Window displays were filled with fake snow and glittering lights and toy trains and anthropomorphic stuffed animals drinking coffee and showing off engagement rings. Who knew how much penguins relished that holiday bling?

Everyone who wasn't trying to park or find their car was in a festive mood. And it was contagious. As in, I needed to remember to take my vitamin C when we got back.

"Funny how cities have their own smell," Jake remarked. "London just didn't smell like Pasadena." He casually dropped his arm around my shoulders, and I smiled at him.

It's not like I needed the physical proof of PDAs, and frankly Jake's willingness to put his arm around me or hold my hand in public meant as much to me as the actual act. I can't deny that warm weight on my shoulders felt good. Right.

"Thanks again for going with me," I said.

"Not like it was a big sacrifice. I like being with you. I never figured on seeing London, so that was kind of nice."

And kind of exhausting. Or maybe that was more my take than Jake's. I'd been the one to push for coming home early.

"If we were to travel somewhere for a real vacation or...something, where would you want to go?"

The arm around my shoulders jumped as he shrugged. "Never thought about it. Kate always wanted to go to Italy."

I glanced at him. His smile was wry, his expression distant. He almost never talked about Kate or their marriage, and I understood that this was out of loyalty to her. That loyalty was just one of the many things I liked about him.

I said, "Ireland maybe? With a last name like Riordan."

"Maybe. Anywhere you're going works for me."

I looked down, smiling, and his arm tightened in a quick squeeze.

We ended up having Irish coffees at Edwin Mills, a hip tavern down an alley off Colorado, which had opened early to accommodate the madding crowds.

Edison bulbs radiated cozy light in the shadowy interior. Fresh flowers decorated the tables, and beautiful, slightly disturbing art hung from the brick walls.

"Any word on when Paul Kane is going to trial?" I asked.

"Not yet. I heard through Chan he's changed lawyers again. He's still trying for bail. Why?"

I shrugged. "Just a crazy morning." The kind of morning where you start reminiscing about all the people who've tried to kill you over the years.

He leaned back in the red leather booth. "What was especially crazy about *this* morning?"

I tipped my finger at him so he understood I hadn't missed the emphasis, and while we waited for our drinks, proceeded to update him re the ongoing battle with the Franchise Tax Board.

He heard me out and then said, "You could hire an accountant to handle the tax stuff, right?"

"Right. True."

"This is not something you need to be stressing over."

"I know." I made a face because he wasn't just talking practicality. He was talking about my commitment to living a healthier lifestyle.

Apparently it wasn't only about avoiding getting stabbed or shot or bitten by rattlesnakes.

Our coffees arrived, but I'd already learned that Jake, unlike me, is not easily distracted from making his point. And sure enough.

"So?" he pressed after I'd fortified myself with a couple of swallows of coffee, whisky, and whipped cream.

"Accountants cost money, you know."

He was unmoved. "So?" he repeated.

I remembered Natalie's "control freak" comment, and sighed. "So I'll see about hiring someone to take over fighting with the Franchise Tax Board."

His mouth twitched in a repressed smile. "See? That wasn't so hard. What was Natalie crying about? Her hair?"

"Her *hair*? No. Although now I'm wondering if her hair is some kind of indicator."

"Of what?"

"That she's turning into a supervillain?" I described for him the full-frontal horror of walking in on Natalie and Angus *in flagrante delicto*. Or *derelicto* in their case.

Jake, far from seeing the gravity of the situation, snorted. "I knew *that* was going to happen."

"You *knew* that was going to happen?"

"Hell, yeah. Sooner or later. And you did too."

"Uh, no. I sure as hell did not."

He looked both unconvinced and amused, which was exasperating. He said, "You seemed to be working hard to keep them apart for someone who didn't know."

I considered the precautions I'd taken, including trying to make sure Natalie was sleeping clear on the other side of the Valley from Angus. Maybe he was right. Maybe I hadn't *wanted* to know.

"She's supposed to be on the rebound from Warren," I complained.

"Exactly."

I shook my head, and he said, once again cutting through the bullshit, "What's the real concern here?"

"Look, I like Angus. He's a good employee, and I think he's a... I think he means well, and I believe he deserves a chance to turn his life around. That said, he's not the most stable guy in the world, and I'm not crazy about the idea of him and Natalie. Who is also not the most stable person on the planet. If she dumps him—and she will—I have no idea how he'll react."

He grunted, which I translated as *I see your point.*

"It's a recipe for disaster." And I couldn't help feeling like I'd been the master chef.

"Maybe. She's right, however. You're trying to close the barn door after the horse has bolted. Hire a couple of additional employees, and you won't have to worry about Angus or Natalie walking out."

I groaned, and Jake ordered two more Irish coffees. He excused himself to use the washroom. I gazed out the window at the rain-dotted blur of wet pavement and old buildings, trying to figure out the best way to broach the subject of Kevin O'Reilly and his missing boyfriend. I knew it would require diplomacy and tact.

"You're tired," Jake said, sliding back into the booth. There was a disarmingly soft note in his voice. "You should have taken today off."

If anyone else had said that to me, I'd have been instantly irritated. Somehow Jake pointing out the truth didn't affect me the same way. Maybe because along with that intimate tone, he was so matter-of-fact.

People got tired and took days off. It wasn't just me or some personal weakness on my part.

"If you were taking it off, I probably would have. Speaking of which, why are we still talking about me? How'd your meeting go?"

He grinned and held up his mug. "I've got a new client."

"That's *great*!" I clinked my whipped-cream-topped coffee mug against his. "Congratulations."

"Maybe I won't have to take you up on that offer of free office space for a year."

My smile faded. "Come on. That's a Christmas gift, not a business arrangement."

"You need the money as much as I do."

Well, no. I mean, yes. But no. I wasn't trying to buy out an ex-wife's share in my house and my retirement. Jake was.

I studied the stubborn jut of his jaw—a look I remembered too well. It was important to him to pay his own way. I got it. Completely. That said, this was something I could do to make his life easier—and therefore mine—so it was a gift to both of us really.

I said, "It's a *gift*, Jake. I *want* to do it."

He looked unconvinced. Into his hesitation, I asked, "What's the case?"

"Missing person. Thank God."

Thank God that it wasn't another cheating spouse, that's what he meant. Infidelity depressed him, which I imagine a shrink would have had a field day with.

"A runaway?" It was a horrible time of year for that—not that there was a good time of year.

"No. Possible endangered adult. The family wants to keep it quiet, so they haven't brought in the cops." His mouth had a cynical curve. "You know the breed. Wealthy West Valleyites."

Uh, yeah. I *was* the breed. Or descended from breeding stock, anyway.

Gradually what he was saying sank in on me. I blinked at him. "Wait. West Valley?"

"That's right."

"A missing adult *son*?"

"Yeah."

I said slowly, uneasily, "What's the name of the family?"

"Arbuckle," Jake said.

CHAPTER THREE

"**A**rbuckle," I repeated.

"Right." Jake was watching me closely. "You know them?"

"Funny you should ask." I was not smiling, though. "Remember Kevin O'Reilly?"

Jake's expression changed, his tawny eyes narrowed. "*That* Kevin O'Reilly?"

By which I deduced the name *Kevin O'Reilly* had already been introduced by Ivor's family, but Jake hadn't connected him to our own past until this second.

I nodded. "That Kevin O'Reilly, yes."

He folded his powerful arms on the table and studied me grimly. "Okay," he said. "Fill me in."

I filled him in. It didn't take long. At the end of my recital, Jake said without inflection, "You told him I'd take his case without talking to me first?"

"No. I told him I'd talk to you over lunch. I didn't make a commitment on your behalf. It's not a done deal."

Not in so many words, but I was guiltily, uncomfortably aware I had come perilously close to doing that very thing.

"No, it sure isn't."

I threw him a quick look. "It wouldn't hurt to talk to him, right?"

"I plan on talking to him. But I can't take his case. I've already agreed to work for the family."

"Well, couldn't you—"

"No," he said with a brusqueness I hadn't heard in a long time. "That would be a complete conflict of interest. The family thinks O'Reilly is involved."

"That's ridiculous. For the record, Kevin thinks the family is involved."

Jake shook his head, instantly negating the idea. "If the family was involved, they wouldn't bring in a private investigator."

"They might. Why *don't* they call the cops if they really think something's happened to Ivor? That's the normal thing to do, right?"

"It hasn't been forty-eight hours, that's one reason. This time of year, the cops are not going to jump without something more to go on."

"To me, it smacks of trying to create a diversion."

He made a dismissive sound. "The same argument could be made about O'Reilly."

"He *can't* file a missing person report. They're not married. He doesn't even live here. The family has to do it." I couldn't believe he was seriously arguing this. "Come on, Jake. Now that you know the Kevin in this is our Kevin, you can't really think he's involved?"

"*Our* Kevin?" He raised his eyebrows.

"You know what I mean."

"You mean *well*, that I do know. From painful experience."

That annoyed me. I can't deny it. The dry, cynical tone paired with his taciturn expression as he observed me from across the wooden square of table…got under my skin in a way that hadn't happened for months.

"Painful experience, huh?" I tried to say it pleasantly, though *dangerously* is probably more apt. Then again, I get those two mixed up. A lot.

Jake's face didn't exactly soften, but recognition flickered in his eyes. "Baby, I don't want to fight with you." His voice was low. The words casual, the tone personal. "I've committed to working for the Arbuckles. Assuming O'Reilly is not involved in the kid's disappearance, ultimately I'm working on his behalf as well. In the long run, he'll get his answers."

I said acerbically, "Answers are useful. What he wants is his boyfriend back."

"Regardless of who pays my fee, there's no promise the Arbuckle kid is coming back to any of them."

There was a stake of holly driven right into the heart of Christmas.

And right on schedule, the Eagles swooped in.

Bells will be ringing this sad, sad New Year's...

Jake was right. I *was* tired. And I didn't want to fight with him either.

I sighed. "Okay, true. But I know I've heard you say that most of the time people who go missing turn up again."

"Correct. However, suicide and homicide rates skyrocket around the holidays. This isn't a good time of year to go missing."

I didn't have an answer to that, and after watching me for a moment, he said, "Do you still want to order lunch, or are you in a hurry to get back?"

What he was really asking was, *how angry and/or disappointed are you?* And while, whether fair or not, I *was* disappointed and a bit irritated, I also knew that tending to this very new and, in some ways, still delicate relationship with Jake needed to come first. It had taken a hell of a lot of time and effort to get this far.

"Let's have lunch," I said, and the guarded look left his face.

We ordered. I decided to try the fish tacos, and Jake ordered the Old Time burger.

We stuck to neutral topics for the next few minutes, and then Jake asked, "Other than fraternization between the inmates, how'd the bookstore do while you were gone?"

I brightened. "Actually, we had a terrific week. This has been our best Christmas in four years."

He smiled faintly. "Congratulations."

"I think the expansion paid off."

"I think you're right." He added, "Which means maybe you could think about taking more personal time next year?"

"Hm."

His lips quirked in the way they do when he's amused but too polite to laugh in my face.

"Maybe start taking weekends off?" he suggested. "Maybe start with Sundays."

"Maybe," I said, still noncommittal.

"It would give you a chance to work on that new book."

That time I didn't bother to respond. It wasn't the first time we'd had this conversation. Making Jake my cardiac rehab partner had seemed like a great idea at the time, and it mostly *had* been a great idea, but it had also resulted in his being a *tad* more tapped into my health regimen than I liked.

I liked having…let's call it *wiggle room*.

Our meals arrived, and as usual I fought the temptation to reach for the salt shaker. English cuisine had proved a serious test of my pledge to low sodium.

"Do you think I'm a control freak?" I asked Jake after a few minutes of thoughtful chewing.

"Not particularly. There are certain things you like a certain way, but in general, no. Why?"

"Something Natalie said."

He nodded noncommittally.

I eyed him gloomily. "Yes. I know. Cloak and Dagger is one of those certain things."

He didn't deny it, just offered that half-smile—quarter-smile?—again.

"By the way, I've got more good news," he said.

"I'm all for good news."

"Alonzo is transferring to San Diego."

Now that *was* good news. Detective Alonzo was Jake's—and possibly my—self-appointed nemesis on the force. He could never quite accept that the only thing Jake had been concealing was his sexual identity. Or that the only thing *I* had been concealing had been Jake's sexual identity. He preferred to believe in convoluted conspiracy theories like…I was a serial killer and Jake was covering for me? Who knows. I don't think Alonzo even knew. He simply hated us both with a passion that was as sincere as it was irrational.

"Why?" I asked.

"No prospect of promotion."

Jake's expression was impassive. I got it. The thick blue wall. Alonzo had committed the cardinal sin of going after a fellow cop. Jake had his enemies, but he also had his allies. And even his enemies disapproved of breaking rank more than they disapproved of anything Jake had done.

From there the conversation moved to the current offer on Jake's house in Glendale—the last two had fallen through in closing. What I wanted to ask him was whether he'd heard from his family, but I knew that if he had, he'd be telling me.

The Riordans had not dealt well with the revelation that their oldest son was gay. Unanimously, they had taken the part of Kate, his ex-wife, even as Kate and Jake struggled to keep their divorce from turning into a civil war.

I had never disliked anybody as much as I disliked every single member of Jake's family. He had done a difficult and painful and courageous thing by coming out. And even if they couldn't support his decision, they could have tried to understand. Nope. It was all about how *they* felt, how disappointed *they* were, *their* shattered hopes and dreams. The Amish could have learned a thing or two about shunning from Jake's family.

Still, the first rule of cohabitation is Thou Shalt Not Diss the Other Dude's Kinfolk. So I kept my mouth shut. Which ought to rank at least among the top three on the Greatest Tests of True Love list, right above the one about spinning flax into pure gold.

Jake finished his lunch—and mine—and then the bill came.

I've got it," he said, and remembering the comment about free rent, I turned my reach into an elaborate raking back my hair. "Thank you. I needed that," I said.

"You're welcome," he said seriously.

While we waited for his credit card to be run, I said, "What do you think about meeting Kevin for dinner? Since you're going to want to talk to him anyway."

Jake grimaced. "From my perspective it would be better not to mix social with business."

I was silent.

He said with sudden, disarming honesty, "And also I would really, really like a night alone with you."

I couldn't argue with that, although I think he thought I was going to because he forged ahead. "I don't care that all the boxes aren't unpacked and that we can't find the toaster or the remote controls or the flannel sheets. I don't care about any of that. I just want a night where we don't have to be anywhere or do anything other than maybe walk the dog and have dinner together."

"I'd like that too."

Jake looked relieved.

"But."

He let his head fall back, looking heavenward. I reached over and covered his hand with mine.

"Hey. I can't blow him off over the phone. Maybe we could meet for drinks. You can interview him, and I can explain why, even though you aren't specifically taking his case, you're still going after the result he wants, which is to find Ivor. And then we can have the rest of the night to ourselves. Which I also really, really want."

His cheek creased in a wry smile. He turned his wrist so that we were lightly holding hands.

"Done," he said.

* * * * *

"Oh, then you *did* come back!" Natalie called sweetly when I arrived at the bookstore. "I guess you're not keeping regular hours yet?" She looked meaningfully at the clock on the mantel.

I opened my mouth to point out that *technically* I wasn't due back until Friday—never mind the fact that I was still her boss and signing her paychecks and keeping her guilty secrets from our combined family, however frustrating to us *both* that was—but the interested gazes of the line of waiting customers decided me against it.

"Cor blimey, Ms. de Vil, don't dock me wages!" I wailed, heading straight for my lair.

I found Tomkins sniffing delicately at the open can of Tab on my desk. "Hey, you're not supposed to be up here." I scooped him off the desk.

He meowed at me loudly, gusting Fancy Feast Tender Tongol Tuna breath right in my face.

It was now unanimous. I got no respect from my staff. Times like these I longed for the good old days when it had just been me, twenty thousand books, and the occasional psycho killer.

I began to go through the stack of messages thoughtfully placed dead center on my desktop blotter. There seemed to be a lot of them, including one from my editor and a couple from my ex, Guy.

It said a lot about my writing career that I was more curious to hear what Guy had to say for himself than my editor.

There were several requests from authors seeking signings at Cloak and Dagger. The boom in publishing meant writers great and small were ready and willing to grab any chance at a signing, even at a small—okay, medium-sized—indie bookstore. Big names like Gabriel Savant and J.X. Moriarity were touching base for the upcoming year, and a host of writers I'd never heard of—including writers who were only published digitally—were requesting time slots. Did they not understand how bookstores operated? Boasting about their Kindle Unlimited stardom was like bragging to me about their current case of bubonic plague.

Thanks, but no thanks.

I decided I still wasn't ready for a return visit from Savant. Sent a *yes, please* to Moriarity, who was gay, an ex-cop, and most importantly, an all-around nice guy who always brought an enthusiastic crowd.

That started me thinking. What kind of stories would Jake come up with if he decided to write a book?

I mulled that over for an enjoyable minute or two and then got busy returning phone messages.

"Can I talk to you?" Angus poked his head into my office as I was getting off the phone after arranging to meet Kevin for drinks at the White Horse Lounge.

"Yep." I pushed my chair back and beckoned toward the stack of cardboard cartons. "Grab a box."

Instead, Angus folded his arms defensively, leaning back against the closed door. "It's my fault."

"It's certainly half your fault," I agreed. "I mean, it's not a matter of *fault*. I know you're both adults, and I know I can't control—don't *want* to control—who you get involved with. I'm thinking of your work relationship and how that's going to affect the store."

At least that's what I kept telling myself was my main concern.

He swallowed, bracing himself for the big question. "Are you going to fire me?"

"No. If I fire anyone—well, forget I said that. I'm not firing anyone. All the same, I'm *not* happy about this."

Like they didn't know that? Like they cared?

"It won't affect the bookstore," he assured me.

"You say that now, but it's already affecting the bookstore. And believe me, I totally appreciate the fact that you worked late on Christmas Eve. Opening an hour late today was not a big deal. In the larger scheme of things."

He viewed me solemnly through the blue lenses of his wire-framed spectacles. "It won't happen again."

"Okay." I assumed he meant opening the store late, though it would have been nice to think he was swearing off my female kinfolk.

Angus said, "I love her."

"Oh God *no*," I said.

He looked startled at this outburst.

"*Don't* start with the love thing," I said. "You barely know her."

"I've been working with her nearly every day for five months. She's smart and funny and really beautiful." He added in afterthought, "And a good manager."

"That's not— That's just— Don't fall in love with her. That's all I'm saying. A couple of months ago she was still moping around over that asshole Warren, remember? She probably still thinks she's in love with him. She's not a good relationship risk. I think she'd be the first—or now the second—person to tell you that."

He smiled at me. A big, wide pitying smile like how could I, an over-thirty bookseller, sometimes amateur sleuth, and an even fewer sometimes sometimes-writer of crime novels *possibly* understand the mysterious workings of the human heart?

As if I wasn't a Master Detective when it came to deciphering the enigma of falling in love against your better judgment.

"You'll see," he said.

CHAPTER FOUR

Jake had left to follow up a couple of leads and was not back when I headed out to the White Horse Lounge to meet Kevin at six.

The place had a nice retro vibe to it. Lots of redwood paneling, velvet drapes, crystal chandeliers, low sofas, and lower tables. It was packed when I walked in. Judy Garland was singing "Have Yourself a Merry Little Christmas," and I felt a funny twinge at melancholy memory. Once upon a time that had been my song. At least during the holidays. Sometimes I still felt a flash of the old loneliness, a flicker of anxiety that I was starting to count too much on loving and being loved back.

I spotted Kevin at the bar. If possible, he looked more weary and depressed than he had that morning, but his expression lightened when he spotted me.

"Hi. You made it."

"Yep. Of course." In answer to his look of inquiry, I said, "Jake's running late. He'll be here shortly. How was your day?"

Kevin looked at me like I was an idiot, and I guess it wasn't a particularly tactful question.

"Were you able to get some rest?" I asked.

"No."

"Ah."

The bartender had her hands full—literally—so I tried to catch the eye of the nearest waiter. He smiled brightly in that *take-a-number-*

buddy! way and turned his back. Okay. Since I was going to have to do this cold sober, I decided to yank the Band-Aid. "Listen, Kevin, a very weird coincidence has come up."

He nodded without much interest.

"Jake has been hired by the Arbuckle family to try and find out what happened to Ivor."

That woke him up. He sat bolt upright, nearly knocking over his beer. "*What?*"

"The decision to hire a private investigator is something in their favor."

I'm not sure he heard me. He looked about as thrilled as I'd anticipated—not that I blamed him. I continued quickly, "The thing is, Jake will get to the truth. He's not going to take sides in this. He'll find out what happened to Ivor, and that's what you want."

"He'll be working for *them.* He'll be in their pay."

"Yes. True. B—"

"And besides, they already know where Ivor is."

"See, I'm not sure that's the case, because as Jake points out, they wouldn't have hired him."

"That's an alibi."

"It's not really an alibi. An alibi would be when someone is—"

"It's a smoke screen. They're building a cover story. They're covering their tracks."

"They don't really have to do that, though, because no one but you is looking for Ivor. Hiring Jake means bringing unwanted attention to something no one has previously noticed."

"When Ivor doesn't show up for work next Monday, people will notice. That's why they have to cover their trail. They're trying to create the very impression you're falling for!"

I'd pretty much suggested the same thing to Jake, so it was kind of trying to have to argue the other side.

I said, "I hear what you're saying, and in fact that thought occurred to me too, but Jake was saying it's pretty unlikely."

"But what does Jake know?" Jake inquired from right behind me, and I gave a guilty jump and nearly overset my stool.

Jake's big hands landed lightly on my shoulders, steadying me—how was it that you could tell someone was amused by the feel of their hands?—as he dropped a quick kiss on the back of my neck. He shook hands with Kevin.

"Long time," Jake said by way of greeting. "Sorry I'm late," he added to me.

"Jake." Kevin sounded even less enthused about this reunion than Jake.

"Iz cool," I said to Jake.

"Sorry to hear about your boyfriend," Jake said to Kevin. Which was a perfectly normal and reasonable thing to say, and yet somehow it sounded sarcastic to me. Maybe because I could hear only too clearly the ghostly echo of Jake from a couple of years ago.

The Jake who used to despise the idea of a normal man having a *boyfriend*.

Kevin nodded curtly.

By that point there were no seats at the bar, so Jake stood beside us, which only added to the general awkwardness of the situation.

I signaled again to the waiter. More urgently. Could he not see that we needed drinks? A LOT of drinks. Posthaste.

Addressing the cosmos in my role as neutral observer, I said, "Kevin has some concerns about how impartial you can be in your investigation when you're being paid by possible suspects in Ivor's disappearance."

"I guess the Arbuckles could make the same argument," Jake said pleasantly.

Not the answer I was hoping for.

Kevin flushed. "According to them, Ivor's not missing. He just didn't want to see me."

Jake shrugged. "That's one possibility."

Unsurprisingly, Kevin had an answer for that, but I tried to forestall it with a quick, "*Okay*. Time-out."

Kevin closed his mouth and glared at Jake. Jake gazed at me with interest.

I said, "Jake, I was thinking maybe you could reassure Kevin on that score by pointing out that you're not interested in taking sides, you're interested in getting to the truth. Because you still think like a cop."

"You think cops don't take sides?" Kevin asked. "Don't you watch TV?"

"You're damn right cops take sides," Jake growled. "They take the side of the victim."

I dropped my head in my hands. Rescue came from an unexpected source.

"What'll you boys have?" the bartender asked. She was a curvy little thing with masses of dark curls and false eyelashes that seemed to have tiny jewels on the very tips. She wore a droopy Santa hat and in fact looked like something teenaged boys asked Santa for. She did not look old enough to drink, let alone serve drinks.

Kevin ordered a White Horse Light. Jake ordered *Laphroaig*, which he and Bill Dauten had drunk regularly in London.

"Black Orchid," I said, and Jake patted my back like that was sort of cute.

Santa's Sexy Helper departed.

"Look," I said, before firing could recommence. "Everybody wants the same thing." Jake raised his brows cynically. "Yeah, but you do, Jake." To Kevin, I said, "And cut the snide comments about cops. You're asking a former cop for a favor."

"What favor am I asking for?" Kevin sounded aggrieved. "He's already working for the enemy."

"They're not the enemy. They're the parents," Jake said.

I didn't even try to intervene that time.

After a couple of minutes, the bartender reappeared. Jake and Kevin paused as the drinks were delivered.

I paid for the round. The bartender moved away, and I said to Kevin, "You're asking to be kept in the loop regarding any progress Jake makes. Correct?"

They both looked at me.

"Well?"

Kevin nodded reluctantly. Jake said nothing, but he did it loudly. I knew I'd be getting an earful once we were alone.

"The most helpful thing you could do right now—"

"Helpful to who?" Kevin interrupted.

I stopped, exasperated, and caught the gleam in Jake's eyes. He was enjoying watching Kevin test my patience, the bastard.

I said, "To *Ivor*," which sobered them both up. "The most helpful thing to Ivor at this point is you let Jake interview you and rule you out as a suspect so he doesn't waste any more time on a dead end."

"All right," Kevin muttered. "Ask away."

Jake said, "Let's hear your story. From the top."

As stories go, it was pretty basic. Kevin and Ivor had met eighteen months earlier while working for a cultural resource management company called the Archeological Research Institute. Kevin was involved in excavations, and Ivor was a paleontologist. They'd moved in together, and for eleven months everything had been great. At least as far as Kevin knew.

The only fly in the ointment was that Ivor continued to be unhappy and hurt about his family's unwillingness to accept that he was gay.

"Uh-huh," said Jake, like he'd never heard of such a thing.

Kevin's own family was accepting of both his sexuality and his relationship with Ivor, so Kevin—by his own admission—had failed to understand how much Ivor's family's attitude bothered him until this holiday season when Ivor had decided to spend Christmas with his family in Los Angeles.

"You argued?" Jake asked. "You disagreed over his coming down south for the holiday?"

Kevin looked pained. "I wasn't happy. I wanted to spend Christmas together. We weren't going to break up over it. It wasn't a *big* argument. I know why he felt he needed to try to make peace with them. His mom's going through chemo. His sister just had a kid. I understood."

"You didn't want to come with him?"

"No, I sure as hell didn't." Kevin's expression grew defensive, and I wondered if maybe it had been a bigger argument than he wanted to admit. "They're all a bunch of pretentious, stuck-up snobs. If he'd asked me, I'd have come with him, but I sure wasn't going to volunteer." He was silent for a moment. "Anyway, he didn't ask."

"When did Ivor arrive in L.A.?"

"The twenty-third. He was staying at the Warner Center Marriott in Woodland Hills."

"And when was the last time you heard from him?" Jake asked. He had a notepad out and was jotting down names and dates.

"Around noon on Christmas Eve. He was going over to his brother's. They were going to play golf."

"Terrill?" I said automatically.

Jake glanced at me. "What was that relationship like?" he asked Kevin.

Kevin shrugged.

"I don't know how to interpret that," Jake informed him.

"Obviously they were getting along well enough to play golf."

"So they usually did *not* get along?"

"They didn't have anything in common. He got along with his sister better. His sister and his mom."

Jake nodded thoughtfully. "So the last time you spoke to Ivor was on the twenty-fourth before he met with his brother?"

Kevin nodded.

"Okay. That's more than I had this afternoon." Jake put his notepad away.

"What did *they* say?" Kevin demanded.

Jake hesitated, glanced at me, and answered, "That Ivor had dinner Christmas Eve with his parents, after which he left for his hotel, and Benjamin and Candace went to a big annual party held by Peter and Ariadne West. They go every year. Ivor was supposed to come over for Christmas dinner with the entire family the following day. He never showed and never phoned. They assumed he'd returned to Northern California."

"They're lying!" Kevin said.

"Why would they assume that?" I asked Jake.

"Ivor and his father argued over dinner. It didn't seem impossible that he might have decided to skip the festivities the following day."

"Wouldn't he phone?" Speaking as a son who occasionally skipped out on family festivities.

Jake turned to Kevin, who said, "Yes, he'd have called."

Jake nodded as though this confirmed his own thoughts. "It seems in character for Ivor to phone, which is why his parents are now, after the fact, alarmed. As someone with experience in investigating these scenarios, sometimes people *don't* call. Sometimes people behave out of character. He may have intended to call, but something prevented it. That's why we have to consider every possibility. Including that Ivor needs time on his own right now."

"No," Kevin said. "We've never gone a single night without talking to each other since the evening we first went out. He would have called me Christmas Eve. He'd have called me yesterday."

"I'm sure you're right," Jake said. The words were neutral, but his too-polite tone sounded like, *What you know means jack.*

That's how Kevin heard it too. His face tightened.

I said, partly to head him off, but partly because I was genuinely curious, "Kevin, you were quick to decide something had happened to Ivor. Technically he hasn't been missing even forty-eight hours. Was there something about this trip that worried you?"

"I just had a bad feeling about it."

Jake finished off his Laphroaig without comment.

"Someone needs to check his hotel room," I said. "We'd know right away whether he really checked out or not."

Jake looked at me and shook his head. It was kind of an *Et tu, Brute?* look. "I've been to his hotel. In fact, that's why I was late getting over here."

"Oh. Right. Sorry." Of course Jake would have the name of the hotel from Ivor's parents and would have already thought of that angle.

"Ivor—or someone pretending to be Ivor—checked out at ten o'clock on Christmas Eve."

I considered this new information. "What do you mean 'or someone pretending to be Ivor'?"

"No one saw him leave. The hotel has automated checkout. The bill was paid online, and his hotel key was left on a nightstand. The room was otherwise empty. His car is not in the parking lot."

"What does *that* tell you?" Kevin demanded.

"It tells me people are busy and distracted on Christmas Eve. It tells me that there's a strong possibility that Ivor checked out early, but it's also possible someone wanted it to look like Ivor checked out early."

Kevin didn't have an answer for that.

Jake looked at his watch. Looked at me.

I swallowed the last of my Black Orchid and said to Kevin, "Try not to worry. It's still really early in the investigation." I looked at Jake, "Right?"

"Right," he said.

If Kevin hadn't been worried before, that grim "right" probably would have done it. Maybe in the end Jake's way was kinder. He didn't make promises, didn't offer false hope. It was a serious situation, and he was taking it seriously. We all needed to take it seriously.

Kevin nodded.

"I'll give you a call tomorrow," I told him, and Kevin's expression lightened.

"Thanks, Adrien," he said with quiet sincerity.

"No, really. We're glad to help." I glanced at Jake. He was frowning, but when our eyes met, his expression smoothed out to one of polite inquiry.

We left Kevin sitting at the table, finishing his beer and staring into space.

CHAPTER FIVE

"**Y**ou want to leave your car at the bookstore and I'll drive home?" Jake asked once we were outside.

The combination of headlights, streetlights, and Christmas lights twinkled in the evening gloom. The cold air smelled like fine dining, car exhaust, and the cologne and aftershave of a million Christmas mornings. It smelled...tiring.

Or maybe that was the jetlag. "Yeah, sure." The idea of sitting back and leaving the driving—and everything else—to Jake was kind of nice. Seductively nice.

"I'll meet you over there. Drive safe."

"See you there," I said.

Given the traffic, I could have walked faster than it took to drive, but eventually I pulled up behind Cloak and Dagger, turned off the engine, and got out. Lights shone cozily from the windows above. I wondered if Natalie and Angus were both up there at that very minute.

That thought wasn't what held me motionless, gazing up at the drawn curtains. I was feeling a strange rush of something like homesickness. The rooms over the bookstore had been my home for a lot of years. My home and my refuge.

I heard the purr of Jake's black Honda S2000 cruising down the alleyway. He pulled up beside my Forester and got out. "Are you going in?" he asked, sounding surprised.

"No. I was just…"

Lurking. Like a creepy relation. That's what Natalie would think if she opened the drapes and saw me down here.

After a moment—and to my surprise—he put his arm around me, pulling me against him and kissing my temple. "We made a lot of good memories here."

Yes. And some not so good memories, but hey, that's part of what makes a house a home. History.

I nodded, leaned my head against his for a moment.

"We'll make good memories at the new house too," I said.

He laughed quietly, a low, sexy sound. "We will. Starting tonight."

* * * * *

He's making a list and checking it twice, gonna find out who's naughty and nice, sang Ella Fitzgerald as we merged onto the I-210.

Jake had my copy of *Ella Wishes You a Swinging Christmas* in his CD player, and for some reason that made me smile. Jake was really not an Ella Fitzgerald kind of guy even if he did sometimes call me "baby," like he was flashing back to his 1950s Rat Pack days.

"So who's Terry Arbuckle to you?" he asked, gaze on the rearview as we outdistanced a big rig truck, headlights flooding our back window.

"Terrill." I sighed. "He was my partner on the tennis team in high school."

He glanced from the road to me. "I didn't know you were on the tennis team."

"Yeah. We weren't too bad either." We'd been unstoppable, as a matter of fact. Until I *was* stopped. Permanently. My heart had been damaged by a bout of rheumatic fever when I was sixteen. Now, however, thanks to the miracles of modern medicine, I had a newly repaired heart valve and was feeling stronger and healthier than I had in years.

"Were you and Terrill—"

"No. God no. I don't think we particularly liked each other. But we were a winning combo, so we sort of hung out. He was definitely straight, if that's what you're asking."

"No." Jake said vaguely, "I know you have straight friends."

Time was I'd have made a joke about Jake being one of my straight friends. Weird. It wasn't that I'd known him so long, but what a distance we'd traveled together.

"Do you think it's possible Terrill had some involvement in his brother's disappearance?" he asked into my silence.

"Is it *possible*? If there's one thing I've learned hanging out with you, anything is possible. He was an arrogant prick, but I never sensed a homicidal streak anywhere but on the court. It's kind of troubling that Kevin never heard from Ivor after that golf game, though."

"Maybe. I didn't get the impression that Ivor was sending minute-by-minute updates."

"You think that's why Kevin was so quick to panic when Ivor fell off the radar? They had more of a falling-out over this trip than he let on?"

"I think so, yeah."

I considered that as the urban nightscape flashed by. Towering office buildings with brightly lit windows. Cars packed tight and shining in parking lots like sardines in a tin. Rivers of headlights flowing through side streets. The occasional square of a park, looking weirdly dark and mystical amid all the concrete and asphalt and metal.

"If something did happen between Ivor and Terrill, that might explain why the family changed their story. It's possible the parents are covering for Terrill now."

"It's a theory." He didn't sound convinced.

"Why would they lie about his still being there?"

"Well, for one thing, they don't like O'Reilly. They blame him for turning Ivor gay."

"*Turning* him? You mean like werewolves *turn* teenagers by biting them?" Emma was a big fan of *Teen Wolf.*

"Simply reporting what I heard."

"Wow."

"They also blame O'Reilly for the strain between themselves and Ivor."

"Yeah, it couldn't be anything *they've* done."

"Again. Merely the messenger."

"Right."

"So please don't include me in those dark mutterings out the window."

I laughed, though it was probably a dark, muttery laugh.

Jake said, "It's possible that if O'Reilly turned up on the doorstep demanding to know where Ivor was, Benjamin or Candace—my money would be on Benjamin—might tell him to fuck off. Or tell him something designed to achieve the same result. If it's true about Ivor not showing up for Christmas and not phoning, they'd be feeling pretty angry and pretty self-righteous."

He had an insider's perspective on that one.

Through the years we all will be together, Ella crooned into the speakers. *If the fates allow...*

I said, "Did you know the original lyrics to this song were 'Have yourself a merry little Christmas. It may be your last. Next year we may all be living in the past'?"

Jake laughed. "Is that true?"

"I read it on Wikipedia. It must be true."

He made another sound of amusement.

It struck me that he laughed more than he used to. But then I laughed more than I used to too.

For a few miles we listened to Ella and the tires hissing on the wet pavement; then Jake said, "Try not to get too involved in this."

"He's a friend. How involved is too involved?"

"He's not exactly a friend. He's someone you helped a few years ago. And now he's looking for more help."

"I could argue that definition, but okay."

"Also."

He didn't go on, and I waited. I could feel him weighing and discarding possible approaches. He said finally, "I'm not working for him. I'm not reporting to him. Before *you* report to him, I have to ask you to consider whether I'd be comfortable with any information you're sharing, before you share it."

The sentence structure was convoluted. His request was not.

"I'm not going to betray any confidences," I said. "I'm not going to betray *your* confidence."

"Never intentionally, I know. But you're sorry for him, and you're sympathetic to his situation. You may feel that he has a right to certain information."

After a moment, I said, "I understand." And I did. My involvement in previous cases had frequently been a source of tension between us. Jake was trying to lay down guidelines for my continued participation rather than try to keep me from being involved. I thought it showed a willingness to compromise on his part—and also a kind of unnerving insight into the way my brain worked.

"Thank you," he said. I don't think I imagined the note of relief.

Somewhereshire—as my teenage crew had called the house I grew up in—was a two-story pseudo-Tudor mini mansion in Porter Ranch. It appeared to have been airlifted out of a fairy tale and plopped down in the SoCal chaparral when the chopper ran out of fuel. There were enough steeply pitched roofs and oddly shaped windows to make up a geometry final. The house, cream-colored stucco and Old World blackened timbers, was surrounded by large front and backyards designed to bring to mind English-cottage gardens. What they brought to my mind were L.A. County water restrictions. Still, no denying it was a pretty house and a pretty yard.

An intimidating black wrought-iron fence surrounded the tiled swimming pool—the pool ostensibly being the reason my mother had "sold" Somewhereshire to Jake and me. Swimming and walking being the two highest rated exercises for cardiac patients.

Not that I was really taking advantage of the pool or the scenic walks provided by the surrounding hills. I did plan to one of these days. Maybe when I started taking Sundays off.

The gates opened, and Jake's Honda skimmed up the cobbled, circular drive. The automatic door rose, and we pulled into the garage.

I got out as Scout, our not quite seven month old German shepherd puppy galloped up to meet us, whining and crying as though we'd been gone another week.

"Why, hello, you poor baby orphan." I knelt to greet him, which was a mistake because he had the brains and heart of a puppy and the body of a very big dog. He hurled himself in my arms, knocking me on my butt, and proceeded to lick my face while airing his grievances loudly.

"*Hey.*" Jake hauled the dog off and offered me a hand. "I must have missed this episode of *Dog Whisperer*. Is that what you call pack leading from behind?"

"Ha. Funny." I accepted his hand and, once back on my feet, brushed myself off.

Jake unlocked the door leading into the house. Scout trotted into the kitchen ahead of us and headed straight to his metal dish, which was empty, of course, though he could have doubled for the Rin Tin Tin of the Silents given the drama and pathos he projected at the shock of this discovery.

Although I'd grown up in this house, it didn't feel like our home yet. Partly that was due to my difficulty in letting go of Cloak and Dagger, and partly it was due to all the cardboard boxes, opened and unopened, covering most of the available flat surfaces.

We were working to remedy that, and the fact remained that it was a very nice house. We were lucky to have it. The kitchen had white, glass front cupboards, blue granite countertops, and glossy, reddish barnwood floors.

There were hardwood floors in the dining room too, as well as a large chandelier of bronze leaves and frosted glass which Jake claimed came from the Vincent Price Collection. Beneath the chandelier was a mahogany Duncan Phyfe-style dining set, complete with china cabinet and sideboard—a "housewarming present" from Lisa, who had conveniently forgotten that she'd already given me a small John Atkinson Grimshaw painting as a housewarming gift. "Moonlight at Whitby" hung between two picture windows which offered gracious views of the large garden and wild mountains behind the house.

The other rooms had plush ecru carpet, fresh white paint over the decorative moldings, and a few pieces of antique furniture from Pine Shadow ranch. A stately set of Palladian windows overlooked the front garden.

As a kid I had taken all this for granted. As an adult, I had to admit it was really pretty much outside our budget if we hadn't had a lot of parental interference—a.k.a. *assistance*.

Behind me, Jake was once again bringing up the subject of obedience training for Scout—another task for all those free Sundays?—and I felt a sudden wave of fatigue like I hadn't experienced since my surgery all those months ago.

"I'll handle it," I said, sorting through the stack of mail we'd picked up when we'd arrived home late the night before.

Bills.

Christmas cards.

More bills.

The next time I tuned back in, he was saying, "...we can have for dinner. We're going to have to pick up some groceries pretty soon. Not that a lifetime supply of Top Ramen won't be handy in an earthquake..."

"I'm just going to run upstairs and change," I said, although running was the last thing I felt like. Or at least had energy for.

Hard to believe that yesterday evening at this time we had been on a plane flying back from England. And twenty-four hours before that we had been *in* England. It seemed like a million years ago.

Scout galumphed behind me as I dragged myself up the stairs to the master bedroom.

More built-in bookshelves, fireplace, and brand new king-size bed, which was another "housewarming gift" from Lisa. She'd picked one of those Hollywood Regency-style beds with a beige padded scroll-style headboard. It suited the room perfectly, but it was not the kind of thing I'd have chosen. Let alone the kind of thing Jake would have chosen.

Here too were more boxes to be unpacked. Stacks of boxes. Mostly books. Books apparently so precious I'd designated them for the bedroom, which had entertained Jake unreasonably. The TV had been set up, but we couldn't find the remote controls.

Scout found his rubber squirrel toy and chomped it invitingly.

The squirrel squeaked heartrendingly, and Scout grinned around its molded form.

"Give me five minutes." I kicked off my shoes and flopped down on the bed. Scout tried to jump up with me.

"*No*," I said, and he settled for resting his upper body on the mattress and dropping the saliva-coated squirrel on my chest.

I tossed the squirrel across the room. Scout watched it go and eyed me reproachfully. "Four minutes," I promised, and closed my eyes.

"*Get off the bed*," Jake said loudly some time later.

I sat up as Scout jumped from the bed. "Just resting my eyes!"

"Not you." Jake shook his head, unbuttoning his shirt. "You're allowed on the bed."

"God. I was totally out." I rubbed my face.

Scout had dropped down to his front paws and was wagging his tail frantically, under the misguided notion I was about to chase him around the house. I sighed, watching him. "I need to take somebody for his W-A-L-K."

Yeah, like Scout hadn't already worked out the spelling of his most favorite thing in the world? He began to do doggie pushups in his excitement.

Jake eyed this performance wryly. "I'll take him. Why don't you grab a nap before dinner?"

"*Another* one?"

"Three minutes doesn't count."

"It does if you're boiling an egg. I don't know what's wrong with me. I never get jetlag."

Jake gave me a quizzical look. "I noticed that."

I laughed. "Okay. Even when I did travel, I didn't get jetlag."

"Take a nap, Adrien. It won't kill you."

"It migh—" A jaw-cracking yawn interrupted me. "Didn't you ever see *Invasion of the Body Snatchers*?"

Jake said, "Sleep with confidence. I'll check the basement for giant seed pods."

"I'm very confident in my sleeping skills. Anyway, that's a wine cellar, not a basement."

"I'll keep an eye out for empties. Bottles or seed pods."

I flopped back on the mattress. "Ten minutes," I told him.

If he answered, I didn't hear it.

"Upsy-daisy," Jake said, interrupting my dream of…Jake. Or, more exactly, Jake's parents.

"What?" I opened my eyes.

It was a relief to wake up. My heart was still pounding hard with all that imaginary rage. Well, the rage wasn't imaginary. The rage was real. I'd been shouting at his father—a man I'd never met. That was the imaginary part.

The room—the bedroom in Porter Ranch—was in soft, toasty light, and Jake was bending over me. He wore the green plaid flannel pajama bottoms he'd worn in London, and he was gently shaking my shoulder.

"Time for bed, Sleeping Beauty," he said.

"Is it? It is?" I lifted my head. I looked beyond him to where Scout was sacked out in front of the fireplace, paws twitching as he went on a long and adventurous dream walk.

"It is," Jake was saying. "Get your clothes off, and get under the blankets."

That sounded promising, although, admittedly, tiring. Foggily, I sat up and pulled off my sweater and T-shirt.

Jake pulled the bedclothes back. "You want the electric blanket on?"

There's something inherently unsexy about the words "electric blanket."

"Huh? No. What the hell time is it?" I peered blearily at the bedside clock, still awkwardly trying to wriggle out of my jeans.

Eleven thirty.

"Eleven thirty," Jake confirmed, going round to his side.

"Wait." I let my jeans fall to the floor. "We're going to *sleep*? What happened to dinner?"

He glanced across at me. "Did you want dinner? I'll heat up your dinner."

"You mean, you *ate*? Without me? You mean, the evening is *over*?"

Why was he giving me that crooked grin? "Afraid so. Yeah."

"Why didn't you wake me? We were supposed to…be building memories tonight."

Jake continued to smile. "We are."

"Yeah, but you know. *Memories*." I half swallowed the word on one of those engulfing yawns. How fair was it that the jetlag lasted longer than the flight itself?

"Because nobody zonks out like that unless he needs the rest." The mattress dipped as he got into bed. He stretched out on his side, watching me fumble the rest of the way out of my clothes.

When I finally slid between the sheets, he reached back and snapped out the bedside lamp. The mattress gave another heave as we crawled into each other's arms. Jake's hair was damp, and his bare skin carried the scent of shower gel. If I'd slept through his showering and getting ready for bed, I really *had* been out for the count.

His arms wrapped warmly around me. Now here was a home-coming. I let out a long sigh.

He kissed the top of my head.

"Night, baby." He sounded sleepy.

"Night, Jake."

But as I lay there listening to the slow, steady thump of his heart against mine, I started thinking about what he'd said over lunch. He was being a good sport about it, but come on.

"I'm sorry, Jake. I really did want this to be just you and me."

"It was." He dipped his head, kissed me between my eyes, which I assumed was a miss. "There's no problem here."

I brooded over that for a few minutes. "Yeah, but you know what I mean."

This time I felt him jerk back to awareness, so I could add sleep deprivation to the list of my sins.

I could tell he was trying to recall my words.

He said finally, a little sleepily, "I do know what you mean, and it's okay. I'm not just saying it. We're together, and there will be other nights and other memories. Right?"

"It needs to be...for once, should be what *you* want."

Silence.

"What?" Now he was awake. In fact, he sounded startled. He raised his head as though trying to read my face in the darkness. "I *am* getting what I want. This is what I want."

"How could it be? London and my family and the bookstore and this house?"

"Baby, what are you talking about?"

"I'm telling you that I'm going to do better, Jake. I'm going to be a better boyfriend. I'll take the dog to obedience class, and I'll try to manage some weekends off. And I won't get involved in any more myster— What the hell is so funny about that?"

He was still chuckling as he kissed me. I could taste mouthwash and amusement and yeah, love.

CHAPTER SIX

"**R**emember, I'm supposed to meet Kate this afternoon," Jake said over the breakfast smoothies.

The smoothies were Jake's idea. I'm not and have never been a breakfast person. Yet I was supposed to believe that he was worried about *his* cholesterol level—come to think of it, that was not unreasonable because once upon a time I'd have been willing to swear egg yolk ran through his veins—anyway, he'd always been a fanatic on the topic of breakfast, and my breakfast in particular.

So every morning it wasn't the weekend or we weren't on vacation, we had a crunchy grain cereal or some kind of smoothie. In fairness, I didn't mind the frozen banana and coffee smoothies and the mixed berry and almond milk ones. *Not* so crazy about any variations on avocado and basil. But love means never having to say *I won't eat that.*

Which brings me back to Kate.

"I remember," I said. "Will you be home for dinner?"

He gave me a thoughtful look, and I said, "I mean, I *know* you'll be home and we'll have dinner. I'm figuring the timetable."

As it was a point of honor for Jake never to discuss his ex-wife, it was a point of honor for me never to ask anything about their interactions. I knew they weren't hanging out these days, let alone getting up to anything that would break my heart, but even the whole civilized, grown-up divorce thing took a toll.

"I don't think it's going to take long. We've got to decide on this counteroffer. I'd prefer to hold out, but she needs the cash."

It went through my mind that this sounded like something that could be handled over the phone, but how would I know? I did know Kate was never going to ask for a favor that he didn't immediately jump to. Including selling the house he'd owned before he met her, at less than market value. And that was okay. Small price to pay for having Jake blend my morning smoothies.

"All right," I said. "If you can pick up the groceries on your way home?"

"I'll pick up the groceries."

"A loaf of bread, a jug of milk, and thou. Also dog food."

"Got it."

"I can grab something for dinner. Thai?"

"Thai's always good."

I swallowed another mouthful of coffee smoothie. "I've been thinking about this job of Ivor's."

Jake rinsed his glass and set it in the sink. "What about it?"

"Is it possible he could have uncovered something on a dig? Something valuable? Something to do with the land itself? Does it make sense to talk to his supervisor at the Archeological Research Institute— *and* doesn't that sound like a made-up name to you?"

"There speaks a mystery writer," Jake said. "It's not impossible that Ivor's disappearance is linked to his job, but it's not the most likely explanation. And frankly, most company names sound made up. Because they are."

"I'll give you the last one," I said magnanimously. "Also the first one, since you're the PI in the family. It wouldn't hurt to contact the institute, would it?"

He considered me for a moment. "You like the idea because it dove-tails with your original meeting with Kevin. It's got synchronicity."

"No. I like the idea because I think it's got possibilities."

"It wouldn't hurt to contact the institute, no. Which is why I've contacted them," he said.

"You already called them?"

Jake deadpanned, "Thanks to the years of training I received simply by watching you solve so many of your most famous cases—"

"Okay. All right. Point taken."

His lip curled sardonically, but his words were grave enough. "The two most likely scenarios in this particular case are accident or suicide."

That was a mood killer. "Kevin checked the hospitals and morgues."

"He may think he did. And maybe he was even relatively thorough about it. But I'll tell you right now that he didn't search widely enough or deeply enough."

"He's not going to have your contacts, that's a given."

He didn't deny it. "He's also going to be too quick and too happy to take no for an answer. The other thing is, the body may not have been discovered yet. We're between holidays. A lot of companies, including city and state agencies, are still closed or running on a skeleton crew."

"And he hasn't been missing that long," I said.

"He hasn't been missing that long," Jake agreed.

"You think he's dead."

He seemed to be looking inward as he said, "I think this can be a tough time of year for people."

I remembered the Christmas he'd told me he was going to marry Kate. The Christmas all hell had broken loose. Literally. Yeah, I'd had some dark moments. No question.

As had Jake.

Neither of us spoke for a moment, and the sunlit kitchen was silent but for the sound of the puppy gobbling down his kibble.

* * * * *

Judging by his Facebook page, Ivor Arbuckle was an ordinary guy living an ordinary life.

He did not look like the kind of person who winds up as a crime statistic on the front page of a newspaper—but that could be said of most of the people who wind up as crime statistics on the front page of news-papers. Me included.

As a matter of fact, he kind of looked like me. Slim, average height, dark hair. His eyes were brown, and he wore scholarly, but face-flat-tering, glasses. He had a nice grin, and he shared it often, judging by the photos of work parties and couple-pics of him and Kevin. He also shared his political opinions, archeology jokes, pictures of his dog, and pictures of various meals.

Kevin's Facebook page complemented Ivor's. More scenes from what looked like a happy domestic setup. Photos of himself and Ivor, photos of himself and Ivor and their dog, photos of himself and Ivor and their friends, photos of himself and Ivor and Kevin's family. His page offered more calls for petition sign-ups, scenic shots, and less snaps of meals.

Knowing the people—or at least one of the people—I was "investi-gating" gave the peeking at social media pages a whole new stalker vibe I'd never experienced when checking out strangers. In fact, this felt a lot more like spying than sleuthing.

And it especially felt like spying when, on a whim, I clicked over to Terrill Arbuckle's page. Terrill's page had last been updated six months earlier. But even an out-of-date page contained a surprising amount of information. Terrill was a VP for Arbuckle Industries, was divorced, had two kids in private middle-school, and enjoyed tennis, golf, and sharing retroactive socio-political opinions with like-minded cronies. There but for the grace of Gay.

I didn't have a Facebook page, so I was not going to judge. Cloak and Dagger had a Facebook page—created and maintained by Natalie—and now and then I appeared in the corner of a photo, looking startled or harassed.

And on the topic of Natalie, she was still not speaking to me.

On matters related to commerce and business, she was communicating through Angus, who looked increasingly nervous and anxious as the day wore on.

I probably looked the same. Fortunately, being out of town for a week had given me plenty of work to catch up on, and it was easy to hide out in the back without having it look like I was, in fact, hiding out.

When Jake was working in his office, we usually had lunch together, but today he was out doing what real detectives did, and I was lunching on ramen soup and a can of Tab at my desk when Lisa phoned.

I knew she had to be seriously worried because for once the first words out of her mouth did not have to do with me or the state of my health. "Adrien, is your sister there?"

"Natalie?"

I must have sounded blank—dealing with the Franchise Tax Board for most of the morning will do that to you, but also it's an excellent stall tactic I've perfected over three decades.

"Darling, the other two are here. *Yes*. Natalie. Her father's very concerned. He's tried phoning her at the house for the past three nights, and she hasn't answered."

"Hasn't she?" I was afraid she'd hear the guilt in my tone. "Yep, she's here. She's fine. Has Bill tried her cell phone?"

"No. You know how he is about cell phones." Lisa sighed. "Is she upset about something? It was her choice not to come on this holiday."

"I don't think it's anything like that."

"What *is* it, then? Bill's very hurt. She *still* hasn't wished him a Merry Christmas."

"I think she's just…" Even I can recognize a life preserver when it hits me in the face. "*Busy.* We are *really* busy right now."

"Too busy to wish her father Merry Christmas?"

"*So* busy. Yes. Don't worry. I'll remind her to call Bill."

"Well, darling, couldn't you simply hand her the phone, and I'll get Bill—"

"No," I said quickly. "No, we've got lines out the door. I'll tell her to call. That would be best."

She made a small sound of exasperation and turned her sights on easier prey.

"And what about you, darling? How was the flight?"

"Fine. Long. I slept through a lot of it."

"That's good. I'm sure you needed it."

"Thanks again for inviting us. It was great. A once in a lifetime experience."

"I knew you'd have a lovely time. And it doesn't have to be once in a lifetime. What about Jake?"

"Jake? He had a great time too."

"I'm glad. It's not easy to tell with him. Are you *sure* you should be back at work so soon?"

"Lisa."

She gave another of those put-out-sounding exhalations. "I know. At least Jake is there to keep an eye on you."

"At least— You make me sound like a recalcitrant toddler."

She laughed her silvery laugh. "Oh, darling. By the way, Bill likes your Jake very much."

"He must, if you've started calling him 'my Jake.'"

More tinkling laughter, like razor blades falling onto piano keys. She filled me in on the wonderful time they were having in the land of my ancestors without us, took me gently to task for bailing on the long-anticipated family vacation, remonstrated with me about not "overdoing"—by now these warnings were so much a part of our interaction I don't think she could have stopped herself if I'd been named Mr. Universe—and finally rang off, after reminding me to get Natalie on the blower to her pop *tout de suite.*

"Bloody hell," I muttered, reaching for the can of Tab.

"Adrien, what do you think you're doing?" shrieked Natalie from the doorway.

Speak of the devil.

Or the de Vil.

I sprang to my feet, dropping the can, and the fizzy brown contents spilled across my desk, soaking the phone messages and tax papers.

"What the fuh—lip?" I yanked the drawer open, grabbing for tissues, and mopped frantically at the soggy mess, throwing her alarmed looks. "What is the *matter* with you?"

She was looking more like a Disney villainess by the moment. Or maybe I was thinking of one of the vampire chorus girls in a Hammer *Dracula* film. Because there was a lot of action on the sibilants as she hissed, "You *know* you aren't sssupposed to eat that. Or drink that. Why don't you jussst empty the sssalt ssshaker down your throat?"

"It's not as filling!" Which, admittedly, was not the most helpful comment, but honest to God.

Oh, but she had not yet begun to fight. "What's the point of having heart surgery if you're just going to waste it all and kill yourself anyway?"

"If you're so worried about my heart, don't creep up behind me and scream in my ear."

"That stuff is *poison. Poison.*"

"Jesus. Do I come unglued when you have a donut? Even after you tell me not to let you have a donut? What the hell." I did more pulling tissues and mopping. After a minute or two, the ill-boding silence behind me registered. I threw an uneasy look over my shoulder.

She was in tears. Like…dissolving into tears. Had she in fact been made of the brown sugar her recent behavior might suggest, she'd have melted at my feet.

"Natalie, what's happened to you? What's going on?"

I don't know if in that moment she reminded me of Emma or I was just finally getting the hang of the big brother thing, but I opened my arms, and she promptly transferred the weather system to my shoulder.

She sobbed out something I couldn't understand. Her whole body was shaking with the force of her crying.

"I don't even drink a full can anymore," I told her. "It was only a couple of sips. See how much there was left to spill on my important papers?"

She shook her head and wept out another unintelligible update.

"Look," I said desperately. "You're a grown woman. I'm not going to tell you how to run your life. If you and Angus want to…you know, I can't stop you. Let's consider the matter closed."

She finally seemed to pull herself together. She drew back and wiped her face—I hastily handed over more tissues.

She blew her nose—a hearty, good blow— tossed the tissue in the trash bin next to my desk, and said calmly, if damply, "What did Lisa want?"

"Uh…" I studied her doubtfully. "Are we not going to talk about this?"

"I'm fine."

"Okay."

"I'm sorry about that. I'm hormonal."

"*Oh.*"

Presumably she had been hormonal plenty of times over the past two years, and I'd never noticed a resemblance to Crazy Jane.

"What did you tell Lisa?"

"Nothing. But you've got to call Bill."

Her eyes widened in alarm. "Why? What's happened?"

"That's the point. He thinks something has happened. He thinks you don't love him anymore."

Her face twisted, but she did not break down again.

Two and half years ago my mother had married Councilman Bill Dauten, thereby supplying me with three ready-made sisters. Bill was a big, bald bear of a guy, and although we didn't have a lot in common, I'd grown surprisingly fond of him over the birthday cakes and family barbecues. I couldn't think of a good reason for Natalie to hurt his feelings over something so dumb as a holiday phone call.

"I'll call him." She sounded like I was sending her to her doom.

"They're worried, that's all."

"Yes."

"And I'm getting worried too. You're not yourself, Nat."

Her face worked, but she stayed in control. "I'm sorry. I know. I'm just going through a lot."

"Like what?" I was astonished to hear myself ask, "Can't I help?"

"No one can help," she pronounced in the kind of tone you expect to use when saying the final farewell to your loved ones in the sepulcher.

I had to give her credit for knowing how to deliver a good exit line. She turned without another word and left my office.

CHAPTER SEVEN

"Did you hear from Kevin today?" I asked Jake over dinner.

I'd picked up a couple of bottles of Singha beer to go with the takeout from Saladang Song, our favorite Thai place. Jake swallowed a mouthful of beer, put down his mug. He speared a bite of shrimp Pad Thai. "No."

"Me neither. I expected to."

"Disappointed?"

My heart skipped, and I looked at him in surprise. He stared back, and for a moment his face looked like a stranger's. Hard. Unfriendly. Come to think of it, not the face of a stranger at all. He looked like the old Jake.

As the thought crystallized, his expression changed, twisted into apology. "Sorry. That was a stupid thing to say."

"Why *did* you say it?"

I thought he wasn't going to answer. Then his mouth tightened as though he was in pain.

"Maybe because somewhere in the back of my brain is the fear that there are some things you can't put right. That I had my chance and I blew it. And that all this"—he nodded at the dining room where we sat—"is just a way station on the road to wherever I'm going to eventually wind up."

It was so unexpected, and hurt so much—for so many reasons—that I felt for a second like I couldn't get my breath. Kind of like the bad old days when my heart had leaked and floundered like a sinking ship.

"Are you saying after everything we've been through, you think this is temporary?"

I thought I sounded steady enough, but his eyes turned dark with fierce, unreadable emotion. His chair scraped back, and he came around to me, folding me in his arms. "Don't look like that, baby," he said softly.

"Because this is *it* for me," I told him, and that time my voice wasn't so steady.

"This is it for me," he whispered against my ear. "Till death do us part. Nothing could change how I feel about you."

I pulled away to scrutinize his face. "You think I might change my mind?"

He shook his head.

"What, then?"

I know he could hear the pain in my tone because I could hear it. It just wasn't possible to hide what I felt for him. Not anymore.

"It isn't logic. It's jealousy and fear. Because I didn't appreciate what I had when I had it. And maybe deep down I don't know that I really deserve another chance."

"Jake. Don't. Don't say stuff like that. Those words don't belong between you and me…"

He pulled me back into his arms, muttering, "Sorry. I didn't mean to hurt you. It's just hard sometimes to believe."

He was holding me so tight it was hard to breathe, like he was hanging on for dear life. I clutched him back. I was pretty sure this—whatever it was—had been triggered by his meeting with Kate and the continued ostracizing by his family.

How could they do this to him? When they knew better than anybody who he was inside. When they had to know how much they were hurting him.

I wanted to fix it for him, and since I couldn't, I wanted to comfort him any way I could. I lifted my face to his and said, "Are you still hungry? Because I don't know about you, but right now I need more than Tom Yum Goong soup inside me…"

The scent of warm, naked skin…

The lamplight threw a summery radiance, kind to the goose bumps, and five o'clock stubble, and shadows under our eyes. Hiding the boxes—and maybe some of the baggage.

It couldn't have been more different from the first time we were together, but something in the way Jake smiled at me made me remember. Like that night at the ranch, he looked a little self-conscious. There was a flush across his cheekbones, and his brown-gold eyes were very bright.

"Have I ever told you I love you?" he asked.

I smiled, smoothing his hair back from his forehead. It was a good face. There was strength and discipline there—also kindness and character. But it was not the face of a saint. His jaw was too stubborn. The line of his mouth was too passionate, too sensual. "Once or twice."

"I love you. I'll love you till the day I die. And afterward. If there is an afterward."

That seemed to go unexpectedly dark. I said gently, "I know. It's the same for me." I angled my head and kissed him. I could taste the beer and hot chili spice as he pushed his tongue against mine. Playful and sexy.

As the kiss came to its lingering, reluctant close, he whispered, "I want you to fuck me."

He might as well have been speaking in Thai. I stared into the fierce emotional blackness of his eyes and couldn't think of anything to say. He nodded at whatever he read in my face.

"I trust you."

My mouth dried. My throat dried. My heart was crowding my chest. "You don't have to prove anything to me," I said at last.

He actually laughed, though he sounded breathless. "I know. It's not about proving something. I want this. I want to share this with you."

Without waiting for my answer—like it was in doubt?—he reached over to the bedside table, yanked open the drawer, and pulled out the tube of clear gel. He tossed it to me, and I caught it automatically.

He got on his hands and knees, which was also...rather basic. But okay. I couldn't help staring at him, and my expression must have been dubious because he said indulgently, "Come on, baby. I know you haven't always played catcher."

No. Not always. But then I hadn't exactly thought of what I did in terms of sports metaphors either. If I had, it would have been something like men's singles tennis champ or extreme ping-pong player.

I squirted a blob of silvery gel onto my fingertips. "Are you sure about this?" I stared down at the shiny glob of lube in my hand, rubbed my fingers, feeling the slick squish, trying to warm it.

His brows drew together. "Don't you want to?"

"Yeah. Of course." Hell to the yeah. Never had I expected it, and certainly not on what seemed like spur of the moment. "It's just— I just—"

"I've thought about it for a long time." Jake sounded strangely calm. Like somebody in a trance state. "I knew if I was going to do it, it would be with you."

It made me smile, but it scared me too because I did not want this to disappoint him, did not want him to do something he would regret, or take advantage of a moment of weakness simply because he believed he'd wounded me at dinner.

I ran my hand lightly over the muscular, round globes of his ass, stroking him. So beautiful. Hard and lean like something wild that had lived alone a long time. His skin felt warm and supple over those hard juts of bone and cartilage. I could feel the pounding of his heart beneath his ribs.

And the pounding of my own.

Jake shuddered. Kind of like the way a horse shudders when a fly bites him. Hopefully more pleasurable than that.

"Did that tickle?"

"Nah. Go on, baby." He sounded more urgent now.

I gently parted his butt cheeks, tracing a finger down his crack—not quite teasing, but not invasive either.

Jake swore softly. It didn't sound like anger, though. Didn't sound like *no*.

Delicately, I brushed a fingertip against the hot, tight—and clenching tighter—entrance to his anus. The nexus? A Celtic knot. My heart was beating so hard and so loudly the thump seemed to fill my chest.

Jake sucked in a breath. His fists and knees punched sharp indentations in the pale sheets and mattress beneath.

"You okay?" I asked.

He threw a quick look over his shoulder. "Yeah. And you're okay. I want to do this. I want you to do this."

Jesus, did I want to do this. I kept thinking of the first time Jake and I had made love. Because even then it had been love for me, even if I had been afraid to admit it.

I continued lightly stroking, and Jake said suddenly, roughly, "That feels...crazy."

"Good crazy or bad crazy?"

"Just…" I heard his swallow, that revealing catch.

I leaned forward, pressing my lips to the heated velvet of the small of his back. Kissed my way up each link in his spine, like the most devoted of priests working his way down the rosary.

With my body, I thee worship.

He gave another of those shivers, said suddenly, "I had to wonder. Your face is so beautiful when I fuck you."

I leaned back on my heels and pressed my finger against the clench. He tensed and then relaxed. I pushed harder, and then I was in. He gasped. I think I might have gasped too. It was intensely, shockingly intimate to do this to him.

His cock was lifting, starting to harden, which was a relief. My own was almost painful in its swollen rigidity. I wanted him so much I felt almost dizzy with excitement and longing.

Jake said quietly, gruffly, "Yeah, that feels good. You touching me there like that. Christ. That's…"

I pushed the oily tip of my finger in and then out, very lightly, giving him friction and rhythm. I knew how good that felt. His sphincter muscle automatically gripped my finger.

I pressed a little farther. Taking my time. Lots of time. And why not. This was pleasurable in itself. I pushed my finger in deeply and continued stroking. Jake moved instinctively into it—he never did anything halfheartedly—and then when he was relaxed enough, I worked a second slick and glistening finger inside.

"Yeah, that's it," he muttered as I sought delicately, experimentally for the nub of his prostate.

Jake sucked in a breath, tensed. I felt the flush of heat on his back, like he was lighting up inside.

"*Chr…ist,*" he said unevenly.

I took the opportunity to slide another finger inside. Jesus, he felt *molten*. So hot, so tight. I desperately wanted inside him, wanted to feel that fierce grip-and-grab down the length of my cock.

I got out, "Okay?"

"Yep," he said in a compressed voice.

"God, Jake," I breathed. "The feel of you."

He grunted. It wasn't distress, but I wasn't sure it was pleasure either.

I eased my fingers out, stroking his back, his buttocks, as I awkwardly, one-handedly slicked my cock. Lots of gel. A ridiculous amount of gel probably.

The head and footboard squeaked as I got into position, resting my hands on his hips, lining the head of my cock against the entrance of his body. He tensed. And I didn't blame him. The age old question: how the hell was Tab A ever going to fit inside Slot B?

And yet it did. It would. I was living proof of that.

I hesitated, though. If he didn't really want it, it wasn't worth it. "Whatever you want," I whispered. "It's always good with you."

He reached beneath himself, briskly, almost impatiently coaxing his cock back to life.

"Come *on*, baby," he said, and for a funny moment I wasn't sure who he was talking to.

I pushed in.

It hurt. I could feel it hurt. I wanted to withdraw, but that would be worse, so I held very still, barely breathing, giving him time to get used to it. Kept my mouth shut because anything would be too much. Jesus, it was *so* hard not to move. That snug, velvet grip seemed to stop time. All that overwhelming physical sensation—his body clasped mine so tightly that every fractional movement sent jolts of exquisite sensation flashing up and down my spine—but it was also the mind fuck of it. Of this reversal. Which would ordinarily not be a big deal, but because it was Jake…was a very big deal.

He shivered and then backed into me.

I couldn't help it. I pushed into him, plunging in farther, then pulling out, rocking against him. Biting my lip to keep from crying out at the sweetness of it.

So hard not to tear loose and go for it. I groaned with the effort, and he whispered, "That's good, baby. So good. Harder."

I could have cried with the relief of that permission. Having come this far—well, or *not* come thus far— I gave a sob, and began to thrust into him. Jake shoved back strongly, and for a few strokes it was humpy and out of sync; then we had it, found a tempo, the beat of a very different drummer.

He didn't try to control or guide it; he simply slipped into the cadence, and it was like driving a very powerful foreign car. Complete with steering wheel on the wrong side.

Racing, almost flying, with no brakes and no seat belt, crashing right through the barriers…sound, speed, light…habit. We were hurtling to an inevitable collision.

My hands were going to leave marks on his hips, and when I spared a look, I could see my cock, pale against the darker tone of his skin, flashing in and out, faster and harder.

I remembered my manners and changed the angle, and I felt the delighted shock of it flare in his belly and roll up his spine, orgasm blazing in his brain and body.

So fast. Too fast. Ridiculously fast. I wanted it to last and last, but he began to come, and I began to come, and the world seemed to explode in a glittering, white-hot mess of broken glass and twisted metal and engines on fire.

The complete and exquisite wreckage of everything I thought I knew. And in its place, something astonishing and new and exhilarating. We collapsed together, a sweating tangle of arms and legs, gasping for breath.

Release had never been quite so…had never felt so much like deliverance. Like religious ecstasy. I felt exalted, and at the same time weak and light, muscles and nerves quivering at the tiny aftershocks of pleasure still zinging through me.

Jake whispered something. I turned my head. "Okay?"

He looked at me, and his face appeared…younger, happy, moved. "Another first," he said.

I let out a sound. I meant it to be a laugh, but it was pretty shaky. He rolled over, hauling me into his arms.

"It was beautiful," he whispered. He grabbed my chin and kissed me, wetly, strongly. "*You're* beautiful."

"Yeah?"

"Yeah. You know it was." He smiled. "You are generous and graceful…and…" He gave a funny laugh. "Christ, you're good in the sack."

I think it was the wondering note that did it. I started to laugh for real, and Jake began to laugh as well.

"Yeah, but it's true," he said.

Not really. That is to say, I knew my way around a mattress, but what made this—well, every time we made love—special, unique, was the intensity of feeling. *His* emotional engagement was part of why he thought it all felt so fucking good. It was funny to me that he hadn't realized that yet, that he was still thinking the difference somehow had to do with my superior technique.

We quieted, and I said, "Jake, what you said at dinner…"

He said, "It kills me when I do something that hurts you. I'm sorry."

"You don't ever have to— There's never going to be anyone else for me. Not now."

"The problem is not you. The problem has never been you. I will get better at this."

"Okay," I said. "I won't stand in the way of progress."

His mouth curved, but it was too gentle, too regretful to form a real smile.

It pushed me into saying the rest of it, although maybe it wasn't the kind of thing you should admit—too heavy to lay all that on another person. "But I want you to know that I'm happy in a way I didn't think was possible. Not for me. I didn't think I'd ever have anything like this. I'm serious when I say if I ended tonight, I'd be sorry for what we won't have, but what we *did* have these last months is worth a lifetime. I can't put it into words, but that's the truth. I would take these last six months with you over sixty years with anybody else."

"Baby." His eyes glittered, and he put his face to mine. Not kissing me, just resting his face against mine, breathing with me. I could feel the flicker of his eyelashes and the heat beneath, the unsteadiness of his lips.

He didn't say anything. But somehow his silence said it all.

CHAPTER EIGHT

Kevin was waiting in the true-crime aisle when I arrived at Cloak and Dagger the next morning.

I can't deny I was relieved. Not that I really thought something had happened to him, but occasionally bad things do happen to people I know. So far not in Jessica Fletcher epidemic proportions, but let's just say that news of the mysterious death of an acquaintance will never take me by complete surprise.

"Where's Jake?" he asked.

"He's got a meeting in Santa Monica. An unrelated case."

He frowned. "I was thinking we would hear something by now."

I had been too, but realistically, missing person cases could drag on for months, weeks, even years.

I wouldn't wish that on anyone, let alone a friend.

I said, "It's tough, I know. Jake's doing everything he can with what he's got to go on."

"What is he *doing*?"

"He's checked with the hospitals and morgues—"

"I already did that!"

"He's using his contacts at the DMV to try and find out if Ivor's car was towed or has been impounded, he's talked to the CHP, he's tried to get access to the security-camera footage at the Marriott, he's interviewed the Arbuckles' neighbors. He's talked to Ivor's boss—"

He had done a hell of a lot in a very short time, but the results had been nil.

Kevin flushed. "This doesn't have anything to do with work."

"At this point we don't know what it has to do with. Which is why he's talking to everybody. And that takes time."

"I've already told you his family is behind his disappearance."

I hung on to my patience. "Kevin, he's not going to take your word for it. He wouldn't be any good as an investigator if he did. He's going to try again to get the family to file a missing person report. Obviously the cops have resources he doesn't, and those extra resources can make the difference. At the very least, Ivor's cell phone records could be accessed, and we'd know where he was when he dropped off the radar."

Or at least where he was when his phone went dead. Because if he hadn't disappeared willingly, his phone would surely be dead by now.

"They won't agree to that."

"Maybe not. They were probably hoping, even assuming, Ivor would show up before now. Now that they understand there's no wishing this away…"

Well, they still might not cooperate.

Movement along the top shelf of the bookcase caught my eye. Something small and beige was slinking our way with sinister purpose. I put my hand on Kevin's arm to move him out of range of my ninja cat, and to my astonishment, he wrapped his arms around me and dropped his head on my shoulder.

"It's the not knowing," he muttered. "I don't know how much of this I can take."

"Uh, sure…" I patted his back kindly.

"*Well!*" Natalie exclaimed, stopping short as she rounded the corner carrying a stack of books.

I made a face at her, complete with eye roll.

She still had the nerve to make a disapproving *humph!* noise.

The front door jingled behind us. Déjà vu. I made a more determined effort to disengage from Kevin's clutch.

Familiar footsteps were coming our way.

"I know," I said, smacking his back more forcefully. "Don't lose faith."

The footsteps came to a halt. A voice from behind me said, "I *see*, said the blind man."

Thankfully, it was only Guy, my ex.

Guy was medium height, lean, with long, loose, silvery hair, a haughty, not quite handsome face, and rather wicked green eyes. The wickedness was real, but only occasional. His loyalty and kindness were consistent.

Becoming aware that a crowd was gathering, Kevin stopped hugging me and stepped back, wiping his eyes.

"Hey, Happy Holidays!" I said to Guy. I might have sounded overly animated. His expression grew more sardonic. "This is Kevin. You probably remember me mentioning him from that time I was staying at the Pine Shadow ranch."

"No, I don't," Guy said. He moved past me to embrace Natalie. "Gorgeous as ever, Natty. I *love* the hair."

"Kevin, this is my good friend Guy. Guy, this is Kevin O'Reilly. He's a— Jake is helping him with a...case."

"A case of what?" Guy inquired. He shook hands briefly with Kevin and turned back to me. "Since you missed my annual Solstice party, I thought I'd hand-deliver your prezzie."

I took the small, silver-wrapped box automatically. "Thank you, Guy. Your gift's still at home in my suitcase." Which was quite true. I'd picked up a 1919 copy of *Spiritualism: The Inside Truth* by Stuart

Cumberland in a weird little London bookstore. It was currently tucked up with my dirty socks and T-shirts.

"Go ahead and open it," Guy ordered.

Kevin, having apparently come to a decision, announced, "I'm going to go talk to Ivor's brother."

I paused mid-unwrapping the silver box. "Wait, Kevin. That's not a good idea."

"I'm just going to talk to him. I can't stand around here and do nothing." He walked past us and out of the store.

"Oh hell," I said, as the door swung shut with another cheerful jingle.

"Some bullheaded relation of Jake's, I take it?"

"Is he?" Natalie sounded surprised.

"No. He's not. Similar physical type is all. His boyfriend is missing, and Jake's helping him. As a matter of fact, Jake's been hired by the family, but it's all the same in the end."

"Is it really?" Guy asked.

"Yes." I finished unwrapping the box. A tiny silver star sparkled on the white velvet lining. "That's pretty. Thank you."

I'm not really much for jewelry, but it's the thought that counts.

"It's an ear stud," Guy said. "It's been thrice blessed. Which is probably the minimum requirement for someone with your aptitude for trouble."

"Hey, I resemble that remark." I couldn't help another glance out the windows at the front of the store. No sign of Kevin. My heart sank. "How's Peter these days?"

Guy looked suddenly weary. "We're reevaluating our relationship."

"Ah. Again?"

His mouth twisted, but he said, "Speaking of former students, and minions of Satan, Angus looks well. Well-fed and well-pleased."

I couldn't help a sideways glance at Natalie, who seemed to be suddenly fascinated by the stack of books she held.

"I'll just put these away," she said, and vanished down the aisle.

"You look well too." Guy sounded wry.

I smiled at him. "I *am* well. Well-fed and well-pleased."

His return smile was faint and rueful. "I'm glad you're happy. I can't understand it, but I'm glad."

"I know you're glad. And thank you for that."

He sighed. "I was going to ask you to lunch, but you're about to chase after that emotional young man, aren't you?"

"Now that you mention it…"

Guy shook his head. "Another time. One hopes."

I caught Kevin about half a block down the street. He was climbing into a red Jeep. For some reason I'd still pictured him driving around in that old Forest Service truck.

Guy was right. He did look a lot like a younger, softer version of Jake. I'd never seen Jake wear that particular expression of relief and stubbornness, though. One thing Jake was not was irresolute.

"This is not a good idea," I told Kevin, reaching the Jeep, slightly out of breath.

"Then don't come."

Since I'd had no intention of going with him, I was surprised to hear myself say, "You sure as hell can't go on your own."

He slid behind the wheel, and I opened the passenger door and jumped in. Kevin started the engine.

"What are you hoping to get out of this?" I closed my eyes as he narrowly missed taking out both a parking meter and a pedestrian—and felt blindly for the seat belt.

"I want to look him in the eyes when I ask him what he did to Ivor."

I opened my own eyes to stare at him in disbelief. "Really? You're now an expert in neurolinguistics? Even if it was possible to tell whether someone is lying from micro eye movements, you charging over there and accusing Ivor's brother—Ivor's anybody—of murder—is guaranteed to create a tense situation and a totally unproductive dynamic."

"If it was you, would you just let it go?"

"No. But I would at least *try* to take the advice of professionals so that I didn't make things worse."

"*How can it be any worse?*" he cried. "He's *gone*. No one knows where he is. No one *cares*."

"I care. Jake cares. The family cares, or they wouldn't have hired Jake. The fact that there aren't any answers yet doesn't mean that no one cares. It means…there are no answers yet. And pissing off the Arbuckles isn't going to get you answers faster." I added, "And if Terrill *is* involved, the last thing you'd want to do is tip him off to the fact that he's under suspicion."

Kevin didn't answer. He was driving with speed and purpose, as though he knew exactly where we were headed.

I said, afraid I already knew the answer, "Have you been to Terrill's house before?"

"I've been staking him out."

"You've been…"

He clenched his jaw. "That's right. I've been watching him. Waiting to see what he does. I know he did something to Ivor. I can feel it in my gut."

I stared at him for a disbelieving moment; then I pulled my phone out and called Jake.

He answered at once. "What's up?"

"Where are you?"

"The parking lot known as the I-110."

"Kevin and I are on our way over to Terrill Arbuckle's."

"Why would that be?" Jake asked with ominous calm.

"Because I couldn't talk him out of going, and I thought it might be better to have a witness." Or maybe simply an innocent bystander. Those usually came in useful for catching stray bullets.

"I'm just going to talk to him," Kevin muttered.

"Goddamn it." The very quietness of Jake's voice made me wince.

"Look, I know. Is there any chance you could—"

"No," he said. "There is not a chance in hell. It's wall-to-wall cars out here. Don't—*do not*—get in the middle of that."

"I'm hoping to be the voice of reason."

"I'd prefer that you were the voice out of range. Way out of range."

"Don't worry. I'm not going to do anything stupid."

His silence was what they call in books "resounding."

"More stupid," I amended.

"Adrien—"

"I'll be careful, and I'll keep you posted." I clicked off.

Sometimes you have to help people avoid saying things they'll regret.

* * * * *

Terrill lived in the Thousand Oaks gated community of Eagle's Nest.

It was not so gated that the security guard wouldn't let us in, but Kevin did have to sign a clipboard and leave his license number. Presumably he'd been doing this on a regular basis if he was "staking out" Terrill, but the white barrier bar raised, and we sped off down a wide, sunny street lined with palm trees and elaborate holiday exhibits that made the place look a bit like Las Vegas off-hours. A lot more reindeer, though.

Most of the homes had been built in the late nineties and went for around a million dollars. They weren't mansions, but they were very nice, and Terrill Arbuckle lived in one of the nicest of the nice.

There were no holiday decorations at Casa Arbuckle, but there was a brand new, shiny Porsche Cayman sitting in the driveway.

"What makes you think he's at home on a Wednesday?" I asked, following Kevin up the curving stone steps that led to the Mediterranean-style front yard. "He's probably at work."

"Arbuckle Industries is closed the week before and after Christmas," Kevin said.

He marched up to the glossy brick-red door and pressed the doorbell.

"Remember," I said. "You just want to talk to him. You don't want to put his b—"

The door opened immediately, which took us both by surprise.

Terrill wore a brown leather jacket and was clearly on his way out to the Christmas-red Porsche.

His glance moved from Kevin to me without recognition.

In fairness, I don't think I'd have recognized him either. He was still blond, still handsome in a blunt, square-jawed way, but he'd filled out, thickened. His features seemed blurred, coarser. He looked a lot like his dad—and every other TV caricature of an evil corporate executive.

"Yes?" His voice was deeper, but I recognized that note of perennial impatience.

Kevin squared his shoulders and said, "You don't know me. I'm Ivor's partner. Kevin."

Terrill's eyes widened. "What are you doing here? What do you want?"

"We want to ask you some questions," Kevin said.

Terrill flashed a quick look at me, no doubt wondering where I came into this—I was wondering the same thing. He said, "I don't have anything to say to you. My family has nothing to say to you."

That was good old Terrill. Never one to waste time on tact or diplomacy.

I said, "Would it hurt to talk to him?"

"Why should I? I don't know him. I don't know you. Why would I want to—"

"Actually, you do know me. We went to high school together. We were partners on the tennis team for a couple of years. And I know Kevin. So could you just take a minute to answer—"

Terrill stared at me. His expression altered. "*English?*" he said in disbelief. He looked genuinely flabbergasted. Did he think I'd died?

It was sort of weird hearing him say my name. I had never liked Terrill, but I realized now that I had unconsciously been a bit attracted to him. Or rather to traits that I now found attractive in Jake.

"That's right, Arbuckle. The Ghost of High School Past. Okay? So you know me, my mother knows your mother, this is all kosher. Answer the guy's questions, and we can go on our merry way."

Terrill was still staring at me like I was indeed a ghost. He said, "Don't tell me you're a faggot too?"

"Don't tell me you're *not* a faggot?" I returned in equal amazement.

See, this is the kind of boyish raillery you're supposed to grow out of, and I'm not proud that I immediately reverted to type. Although it was a pretty good shot, and it hit him right where it hurt the most. He went red, and then he went redder.

It wasn't productive, though, and it got less productive when Kevin shouted, "I want to know what you did to Ivor!"

"What the fuck are you talking about?" Terrill roared back. "What I did to— How fucking dare you?"

Impulse control had never been his strength—on or off the court—and nothing had changed. He shoved Kevin, who staggered back a couple of steps, but then charged forward again.

"The hell, you two." I lunged, trying to get between them.

Not all instinct is good instinct. Standing between two muscular males trying to pulverize each other is never a safe place to be, and I was pretty sure I was going to get punched in the face, at the least—which would not be nearly as painful as listening to what Jake would have to say about this.

"Are you assholes *kidding* me?" I gasped as we bear-hugged our way around Terrill's doorstep.

"What did you do to him?" Kevin kept yelling. Mostly in my ear.

"You come here and accuse me of hurting my brother? My own brother?" Terrill yelled back. Mostly in my face.

"This isn't *helping*!" I also yelled. To anyone who would listen. Which was nobody.

I think it probably would have ended with all three of us falling off the door stoop, cannon-balling down the driveway, barreling down the street, and winding up at the guardhouse—and eventually in jail—but rescue arrived in the form of the neighborhood security cruiser.

Three short *whoops* of a very loud siren had Terrill and Kevin breaking their death-grip on each other—well, mostly on me—and retreating to opposite sides of the small Cyprian oasis front yard.

"You're the last person who saw him." Kevin was still ranting. "I know you did something to him."

"You're crazy," Terrill snarled back. "He was trying to get away from *you*."

"We're leaving," I called to the rent-a-cop, who had climbed out of his car and was trying to figure out how to undo the side guard on his holster.

"Time to go." I grabbed Kevin by the back of his collar and steered him toward his Jeep.

He didn't fight me, didn't protest, stumbled along silently, and I realized he was crying or close to it.

I was sorry for him, but I couldn't find any words of comfort. For either of us.

CHAPTER NINE

"**I** thought my being there would help defuse the situation."

"Fine." Jake took a time-out in his pacing up and down. Although, it was more like circling. Like the room wasn't big enough for him. Or maybe for both of us. "Next time, you leave the defusing to the bomb squad. You leave it to me. I don't care who you leave it to, but *you* stay out of it. You're doing all you need to do. I don't want you any more involved than you are."

Two hours after the impromptu brawl at Terrill's, I was in Jake's office—sitting on his desk, to be precise—for our debriefing. Also known as getting chewed out. The part that really hurt was I knew Jake was mostly in the right. "Come off it. You couldn't get over there in time, and there wasn't any need anyway."

"Adrien—"

"I'm not talking about running my own investigation. I know these people. Sort of. I thought I could be of use—"

Yeah, not so much. Although it might have been worse if Kevin had gone on his own. I wasn't sure.

Jake cut in, "You know why not. Because during the past six months you've had a couple of heart attacks and you've had open heart surgery."

"They weren't really heart attacks. It was just getting shot—"

Jake said, "Yes. You were shot, and you suffered a series of small heart attacks. Right? So no bullshit about it."

"Right," I said very quietly. Weird how my chest tightened hearing those two little words. Heart. Attack. He was right. That was the truth, whether I liked hearing it, whether I liked admitting it. The doctors believed the damage had repaired itself and that my heart was in pretty good shape, but maintaining the status quo required what they drolly referred to as "a lifetime commitment to heart health."

Keyword: *lifetime.*

"You're so goddamned lucky. And you don't realize it."

"I *do* realize it." Despite my efforts to keep cool, I was annoyed. "You think I don't know how lucky I am?"

How the hell could I miss it when everyone pointed it out so regularly?

"You're healthy. The healthiest I've ever known you. And that's how I want it to stay. I want you around for a long, long time. I want to spend the next fifty years with you. I'm *counting* on spending the next fifty years with you. So please, for the love of God, don't do anything to mess that up for us. Not everyone gets a second chance."

"I *know* it. Jesus, Jake. You don't have to make me feel..."

"Go on," he said tersely.

"I know what you're saying, and I know why you're saying it. You love me and want to protect me. I'm not— I also don't want to waste— I want there to be some point—" I stopped because there are some things that are hard to talk about even to someone I loved and trusted as much as I did Jake.

I think he understood because he said, "The last thing I want is to make you feel ill or helpless. You're not. But you're not invincible either. If you look for trouble, you'll find it. You always do. Hell, you find it when you're *not* looking for it."

Your aptitude for trouble.

Guy's Solstice gift was a sudden weight in my pocket.

I stared at Jake and for the first time saw the lines of worry and stress around his eyes. Saw the shadows in his eyes. Saw that this wasn't about territory or trespass. That it wasn't about winning an argument for the sake of being right.

I said wearily, "Okay."

Jake studied me narrowly. "Okay?"

"Yes. Okay. You're right. I should not be taking dumb chances. Especially if I'm taking them just to prove to myself I'm not afraid to take them anymore."

I don't know if he followed that or not. I was still working out what I was trying to put into words. I didn't want my gratitude for having a chance at a normal life to make me afraid to live that normal life?

Not like amateur sleuthing was anyone's definition of a normal life.

Though surprised at my capitulation, Jake was never slow to press his advantage. "And as for Kevin, the best thing he could do right now is go home."

"He's not going home."

"He's not helping by staying here."

"I wouldn't leave if *you* went missing."

Jake's eyes seemed to darken. He said gruffly, "Okay. I'll give you that one. And if you could manage to keep him from getting in the middle of my investigation again, *that* would genuinely be helpful."

I cupped my hand to my ear. "Wait. I didn't catch that last word. Did I just hear you say my involvement would be *helpful*?"

His lips twitched. "Smartass."

I was leaning forward to kiss him when *tap, tap, tap*!

Someone rapped on the door frame of Jake's office. Jake straightened so fast I'm surprised he didn't throw his back out. I glowered at Natalie, who was hovering in the doorway, looking apologetic and defiant.

"Yes?" I said.

"Can I talk to you?"

I've never had a girlfriend per se, but I've had several girls-who-are-friends in my life, plus I've now got three sisters, and I speak with confidence when I say if a female says *Can I talk to you?* in that high, wavery voice, there is trouble ahead.

Big trouble.

I stood up. "Did you call your dad? What's wrong?"

Natalie's blue eyes flicked from me to Jake.

Jake said, "You want me to leave?"

"It's your office." I asked her, "Do you need to talk to me downstairs?"

She shook her head. "You may as well both hear it. There isn't going to be any hiding it."

"What it?" I said uneasily. "It what?"

She threw a quick look down the hall, like she thought her enemies were closing in, then stepped the rest of the way into Jake's office and closed the door. She leaned back against it.

"I'm pregnant," she said.

"*What?*"

She repeated in that scared, slightly hostile tone, "I'm pregnant."

"*How?*"

I felt Jake look at me, and I said, "Okay. I know how. I mean…*who?* It can't be Angus. Not this fast."

"It's not that fast," Jake said quietly. "Is it?"

It was my turn to look at him. He was studying her with that closed, slightly cynical expression—what I thought of as his "cop face."

"No," she admitted. "It's been—we've been—for a while."

"How long a while?" I asked faintly.

"Two months."

"Two..." I sat down on the desk again.

"So whose kid is it?" Jake asked. "Warren's or Angus's?"

Her face crumpled. "I don't know! It could be either. Either of them could be the father."

"What the hell," I said. "How the hell old are you? Didn't you take precautions?"

She began to cry. But it is the gift of Shaolin master girl arguers to cry and fight at the same time. "Of course I took precautions! Most of the time. That's not the point!"

"*Most of the time?* How *most of the time* could it have been if *two* guys could be the father?"

"Okay," Jake said, and that was definitely his cop voice. *Break it up, people. I don't want to have to arrest my boyfriend.*

"And speaking of fathers," I said, "have you told Bill? Have you told Lisa? Have you told Angus?"

Jake put a hand on my shoulder. Natalie burst out, "I'm telling you first!"

For some reason, that disarmed me. Also the fact that she didn't just look scared and angry, she looked so *alone,* pinned against the door.

I shoved down my own anxiety and alarm, rose from the desk, and walked over to her, and I guess I looked suitably sympathetic because she howled, "Oh, Adrien, what am I going to *do?*" and hurled herself into my arms—much like Scout did when he was feeling the world was too much with him.

"Don't look at me. I have NO idea," I said. Thankfully the words were only in my head and not in the surrounding airspace.

"Are you keeping it?" I asked.

She nodded her head against my shoulder. I felt a greater weight settle on me because I knew without a doubt this was about to become my fight. I was going to have to intercede with Lisa—maybe even with Bill—and I might have to intercede with Warren and/or Angus, depending on what kind of role she wanted or they wanted. *A baby.* I could think of nothing more terrifying. Then another weight settled on me—Jake's arms wrapped around me and Natalie both in a rough group hug—only this weight was more of a supporting beam.

Here was help and support for me and Natalie *and* this unborn kid.

Natalie was saying, "I couldn't talk to Daddy until I knew what I was going to do. If I was going to keep it or not. But I do want it. I don't care about the rest of it. I won't give it up. I know it's going to be a mess with Warren—or Angus. Whichever."

"Probably both," I couldn't help saying.

Jake gave me an extra squeeze.

"So you can't fire me. I need this job…"

"I'm not going to fire you." Oh God. I was going to have to give her a pay raise.

"And if Angus gets weird about this…"

"He's not going to get weird." Yeah, he probably would get weird. "You're going to have to tell him, though. Like today."

"Warren's going to want me to get rid of it."

Jake growled, "Warren can go fuck off." Which wasn't elegant, but pretty much summed up my feelings.

"Daddy's going to be so disappointed. Lisa will be disgusted."

Oh God.

I took a deep breath. "I'll talk to Bill and—"

"No," Jake cut in. He sounded sympathetic but firm. "This is Natalie's call. Literally Natalie's call to make. You can swoop in later with the diplomacy and tact, but Natalie's going to be a mom, and she needs to establish her position now."

He quit hugging us, and we all took a step back. Natalie wiped her face and nodded. "I guess so."

"Yes," Jake said. "Anyway, Adrien and I are going out of town this afternoon."

I looked at him in surprise. "We are?"

"I got Ivor's probable return route from O'Reilly. I want to try following it, and I thought you'd like to come. I figure on spending the rest of today and probably most of tomorrow on the road."

No way did I want him going without me. Though it was kind of short notice for my already frazzled staff. "It's hard for me to leave just now."

"You weren't even supposed to be home until Friday," Jake pointed out. He stared meaningfully at Natalie.

She looked blank and then said, "Oh. He's right, Adrien. Anyway, it's okay. It's quiet today. I'll talk to Angus." She sighed. "And Daddy." Bigger sigh. "And Warren."

"Is there a rush on talking to Warren?"

Jake gave me a disapproving look, and I shrugged. "Okay. Yes. Warren deserves a heads-up too. I suppose."

"I'll take care of it. All of it," Natalie said bravely.

"Okay," I said doubtfully.

"Good. Settled," Jake said.

Natalie continued to look brave.

I said, "Well, right. Then when Jake and I get back, we'll figure out...things. Don't worry. Whatever happens, you've got our support."

"Yes, you do," Jake said.

She smiled—the first real smile I'd seen from her since we'd got back from London.

* * * * *

"Why the sudden decision to follow Ivor's escape route?" I asked.

Jake and I were on our way back to the house in Porter Ranch to pick up the things we'd need for our impromptu overnight trip. The skies were blue and the freeway relatively empty, which is about as good an omen for travel as you'll get in this state.

"I mean, aside from wanting to put space between me and Kevin," I added.

Jake's cheek creased in a not-quite-smile. "Kevin's taking the alternate route," he said.

"Ah. Is that metaphorical or—"

"He's driving Ivor's possible alternate route home."

"So you just want my company?"

"I do want your company, yeah," he returned quite seriously. "Always. As far as why we're making this trip? Because the Arbuckles followed my advice and filed a police report, but the cops are not moving aggressively on it. For the very reasons I was afraid of. A guy deciding to take a breather from family and loved ones after a falling-out with said family and loved ones is pretty common. Especially during the holidays. If Ivor still hasn't turned up next week, they'll jump into action."

"Next week could be too late."

"Yes. Today could be too late, frankly."

That was a depressing thought. Jake's profile was stern behind his dark sunglasses.

"What about accessing his phone records?" I asked.

"The cops don't believe they have probable cause. Not at this juncture."

"Great. By the time they do, that phone will be dead."

And maybe Ivor too.

Ella Fitzgerald filled in the silence with "What Are You Doing New Year's Eve?"

Here comes the jackpot question in advance...

Kind of strange—a good strange though—to think that for the first time in recent memory I actually knew who I'd be spending New Year's Eve with.

"Also," Jake said, and his tone was brisk, "I thought Natalie should have some space right now to figure out what she's doing."

"You think I'd try to interfere in her decision-making?"

He smiled, although the smile seemed to be at his own thoughts. "My greater concern is her guilting you into fighting her battles for her."

"Whereas you'd prefer to fight them," I said dryly.

"I don't mind fighting her battles if she really needs help," Jake said. "I don't mind fighting your battles. You fight your own battles, though, so I'd have to fight you first."

"This is getting complicated."

He threw me a sideways look. "Sometimes it is complicated."

I smiled out the window, but then remembered my original point. "So now you do think Ivor might have started home and run into trouble?"

He said slowly, "Did you believe Terrill when he said he had nothing to do with his brother's disappearance?"

"Yes. I did."

"And I believed the parents when they said Ivor came to dinner Christmas Eve and there was an argument. I've exhausted every reasonable lead on this end, so I think it's safe to assume Ivor did decide to skip Christmas with the folks and head back to NorCal. It was late at night, it was raining like hell, and it's a long drive. There are a lot of lonely stretches where, if he went off the road, it might be a while before anyone noticed."

I had a swift, sharp recollection of driving the dark and winding curves of Angeles Crest three Christmases back and thinking something very similar. The bad old days. The bad old nights.

Hard to believe that I was sitting here next to Jake now.

Jake said, "And the final reason I asked you along is I really do need your help." I couldn't see his eyes behind the sunglasses, but his smile was for real.

I smiled back.

CHAPTER TEN

Kevin and Ivor lived in the city of Angels Camp, in Calaveras County in the High Sierras, which—depending on the route and traffic—was supposed to be about a six- or seven-hour drive from Pasadena. It took Jake and me six hours just to get to Fresno.

We checked every rest stop, every truck stop, every service area and scenic overlook. We touched base with local sheriff departments and police stations.

Kevin was driving the I-5 and making a lot better time than we were on the CA-99.

"He's not taking enough time to really check," Jake commented the last time I got off the phone with Kevin. "He's just driving the normal route. Maybe checking rest stops. He's not thinking about what Arbuckle might do if he was too tired to drive, or got lost, or had a flat tire, or needed to stop for coffee, or use the toilet."

I understood what he meant. "If he'd had an accident along a major highway, we'd know about it. Even if he'd had to abandon his car for some reason, by now the registration plates would have been run and the family or Kevin would have been notified."

"Exactly." Jake's glance was approving. "Whatever happened to Arbuckle happened off the main highway, which is why his vehicle hasn't been discovered. And it most likely happened outside L.A. County."

I hid a smile at this blatant bias on behalf of SoCal law enforcement. "Do you think it's possible he decided to walk away from his life?"

Jake seemed to think it over. "It does happen. And when it happens, the family is always as surprised as everyone else. Usually there are indicators. They may only be visible in retrospect, but they're there. I'm not seeing any sign of that here. Granted, it's still pretty early in the game. The kid's only been missing four days."

"He's not really a kid. He's twenty-nine."

"He's a kid to me." He smiled faintly. "You're a kid to me."

"You must be counting in cop years."

"Maybe."

"At least you can't claim you're old enough to be my father." I glanced at him with exaggerated unease. "*Can* you?"

His mouth curved into a reluctant smile. "I was sexually precocious. I wasn't *that* sexually precocious."

"Whew!" I mopped my forehead.

The light was failing by the time we reached Fresno, and Jake called off our search for the night.

The temperature had dropped to the low fifties, and it was windy and very cold when we finally booked a room—a cabin, to be precise—at a motel called the Rustic Inn. "Rustic" seemed pretty accurate. The place was right off the highway, but surrounded by a wall of Ponderosa pines that created the illusion of remoteness. The mint green paint and peeling white trim looked original 1950s—as did the elderly lady behind the reception desk. But you can't go by appearances. The motel had earned a four-star rating on my phone app.

Granted, you can't always go by phone apps either.

We'd skipped lunch in an effort to make the best possible time, and we headed straight for the adjoining coffee shop. Giant white and blue snowflakes were painted on the large windows. A ribbon of old-fashioned Christmas lights was strung along the eaves. A handful of customers—most of them looked like locals—were partaking of the evening's special: turkey meatloaf.

"I think I'm going for the BLT," I told Jake. "I don't trust anyone serving turkey four days after Christmas."

"Ah. Bacon. The forbidden fruit. Yeah, BLT sounds good."

I gazed at the nearly empty parking lot from beneath the edges of a giant snowflake. "I wonder how Natalie's doing."

She had called a couple of hours earlier to say she had spoken to Bill and Lisa. They were not taking the news well, although neither had tried to argue her out of keeping the baby.

"She'll be okay," Jake said. "I think this might even be good for her."

"An unplanned pregnancy?"

Blood heated my face as I heard the echo of that. I said, "I mean, I know it happens and it can work out. For the best."

Jake replaced his menu in the holder. He said neutrally, "Every situation is different."

I nodded. Glanced at him. His expression was closed. I stared back out the window. What had we been talking about before my idiot comment? I was blanking.

Jake said quietly, "It's not an off-limits topic."

"No, I know."

Mercifully, the waitress appeared to take our order. She departed, only to appear again with our soft drinks. When she departed the second time, I said, "What did you and Kate decide about the house?"

Jake pulled the paper off his straw, rolled it into a pea-size ball. "We've accepted the lowball offer. She's got a new job back East, so she really does need the cash."

Now that was news. I stared at him. "A new job? What new job?"

He laughed.

"What's funny?"

"You know that sheriff's position I considered taking in Vermont? They hired someone else for the job, but it didn't work out, so Kate applied."

"She got the job?"

"Yep." He looked…proud.

"So she's moving to Vermont?"

He nodded.

"That's news." Why did I feel so relieved? It wasn't like Kate was a difficult and demanding ex. There were no kids to tussle over, and they didn't squabble over money.

"How do you feel about that?" I asked.

"I feel like it's a good fit for her. She deserves this opportunity. She'll make a great sheriff. And starting fresh is…smart."

I asked—reluctantly, because this was something I really didn't want to know, "Has it been hard on her?"

"It's been hell for her." His tone was flat.

I thought that unplanned pregnancy might not be off-limits, but this sure was.

Jake surprised me, though, by adding, "It helps that Alonzo's leaving, but it's not enough. She needs a complete change of scenery."

I nodded. "I'm sorry."

He shook his head. "No. This is all on me. Which is why I want to do anything I can to make life easier for her—without making life harder for you. Does that make sense?"

"Yes."

"As for Natalie's pregnancy—it'll work itself out. Maybe not the way either of us would like, but it's her life."

"I know."

"To be honest, I kind of like the idea of a kid being around. I like kids."

No news there.

"You'll probably be the closest thing that baby will have to a father," I said. "Given Natalie's track record with relationships."

He snorted. "She might surprise you. Angus might surprise you. Either way, I think you'll play a significant role in that kid's life."

If he was trying to cheer me up, he was on the wrong track. "I'm not good with kids."

"You're great with kids. Emma idolizes you."

"Oh, well, *Emma*," I said, which he seemed to find funny.

The BLTs turned out to be pretty good—and the fresh made pumpkin pie the waitress talked us into after our meal, was even better.

Jake suggested a walk, and though the night was cold and the moon only a slip of silver crescent behind hazy clouds, we did a couple of laps down a deserted stretch of highway adjacent to the freeway.

It was still early, but it had been a long day, and I was glad when we finally turned in. Our cabin was a bit chilly, but as clean and Spartan as a monk's cell. I'm guessing we passed the time a bit differently than most monks.

Jake had come prepared with a stocking-stuffer lube—I was afraid to ask who'd gifted him that one—called Climax Bubbles. The small "sensation" bubbles popped and snapped as he worked the gel into my hole with those strong, sensitive fingers. A couple of minutes in and I was gasping and squirming in the thin, bleach-scented sheets, trembling on the edge of orgasm from that skillful touch alone.

"Jesus, Jake," I panted. "I can't hold out…"

His voice was hot against my ear. "Surrender, baby." And his fingers did a little twist that sent tingles shooting through every molecule in my body. I arched up into his arms and came so hot, so hard, it was practically an explosion.

I collapsed against him, moaning, "What the... I think I lost brain cells that time."

His chuckle was deep and sexy. "I'm sure your family thinks you've been losing brain cells since you met me."

Yeah. Which was nothing to what his family probably thought of our brain power combined. However, I wasn't about to ruin the mood—if you could call erotic reverie a mood.

"Got your breath back?" he teased after a few playful minutes of tweaking my almost painfully sensitive nipples.

I shifted at the nudge of his cock, and his arm locked around my waist, lifting me and then settling me dead center on the head of his shaft. "Oh, *Christ*." His voice was deep, guttural as his hips thrust up, neatly impaling me.

A helpless sound of pleasure escaped me. My body was so used to accommodating his now. We were a perfect fit. Like a powerful hand reaching into a well-worn glove, smoothing out the kinks and creases, stroking the rough patches till they were silky soft and soothed.

Better to give than receive? Maybe not. Not when receiving was this good.

"I can't help it," he muttered, thrusting into me. "I just...want you... all the time..."

"Jake. Jesus. Jake."

"Yeah, that's it. That's it."

I pushed back into those brisk, rhythmic strokes, contracting muscles, working for it together.

The bed was jerking so hard the wooden floor squeaked loudly beneath. Sort of comical, in a distant way. The shade on the lamp was bobbing back and forth, a gray shadow in the firelight.

Memories to be squirreled away for later. Already so many memories.

So. Good. So. Good. So. Fucking. Good.

I bore down hard and felt his body seize. He began to come hard, hot wet seed flooding my channel. The sweaty, sticky, sweet messiness of sex. Of love.

He pulled me to him. I wrapped my arms around him.

Not a "big" night. Not a night of "firsts". Every kiss, every caress didn't stand out in my recollection. Nothing memorable was said. Just a regular old ordinary night—I was looking forward to a lifetime of them.

* * * * *

We were having breakfast at a place called the Nickel and Diner when Jake's cell phone rang.

We were expecting to hear from Kevin, so I don't think he even looked before he clicked to answer.

"Riordan."

I could tell at once from the way his expression went from business-like to stony that it wasn't Kevin. He put down his fork.

"Uh-huh."

What seemed to me to be a very long silence followed. I put down my fork too. He met my eyes once, then looked away, and my heart seemed to squeeze at the darkness I saw there. It wasn't all anger. There was a lot of pain—genuine hurt—in that bleak gaze.

I swallowed my coffee and stared out the picture window at the pine trees and mint green cabins.

"Saturday," Jake said. "What time?"

Silence.

"And this includes Adrien?" He met my gaze again, but this time I couldn't read anything.

"We're in Northern California right now. I can't say for sure. I appreciate the invitation, though."

The pause that followed was shorter. "Yeah," Jake said. "Love to Mom."

He clicked off.

"Was that—"

"That was my father. We're invited to New Year's Eve at my parents'."

"Oh," I said, because nothing else came to me. I thought this was probably a very big deal. If Jake had spoken to anyone but his mother since he'd come out to his family, I was unaware of it.

He didn't look like it was a big deal. He looked cold and withdrawn. Zero emotion now.

"Are we going?" I asked.

His gaze, hard and shiny as agate, met mine and seemed to soften. He even gave a twisted kind of smile. "Don't we have plans?"

"Well, not really. We have a number of options. I haven't committed to anything. I was kind of thinking we might play it by ear."

He shook his head.

Which was a relief. I had no desire to meet Jake's former loved ones. Wasn't sure how polite I could be with the people who had convinced him for forty years that he was sick and perverted—who undoubtedly viewed me as sick and perverted—who were a big part of what *had* fucked him up so thoroughly.

Except.

They weren't Jake's former loved ones.

He still loved them. I couldn't unsee the hurt and anger that had been in his eyes while he'd been speaking with his father. Nobody has the power to destroy you like people you love.

I said, "The thing is, this is an olive branch. They're reaching out to you."

"Are they?"

"Yeah, Jake. They are. They don't want to start the New Year at war with their oldest son. Or their big brother. I think that's…good." What I actually said was "guh." I'd been trying for something more enthusiastic, but "admirable" stuck in my craw and came out as a *guh*.

'Cause, yeah. *Guh* was how I really felt.

But this wasn't about what I felt. It was about what Jake felt, what he needed. And he needed them. Not all the time, and not in all ways, but a part of him did need something from them.

And they deserved…a second chance.

Everyone deserves a second chance.

He continued to eye me in that grim, sort of pained way. "It's not a real party. It's just family. They're not like your family," he said.

"So there's a point in their favor."

He didn't smile. "I'm serious. They're not… You're not going to have anything in common with them."

"I have *you* in common with them. And who cares? We're not moving in with them. Anyway, you really do underestimate me. I can be *very* charming when I need to be."

"I know."

I laughed. "And that's what worries you?"

His lips tugged into a reluctant smile. "No."

I tipped my head. "Come on, let's meet them halfway. If it doesn't work out, well, next year we do something else for New Year's. Something that doesn't involve broken beer bottles and jail time for your mom."

He snorted. Picked up his coffee cup. "I'll think about it."

"Don't think about it *toooo looooong*," I trilled softly. "I have to pick my *outfit* and get my hair *done*!"

Jake choked on his coffee.

CHAPTER ELEVEN

I don't think I really believed we would find the car.

For some reason, I had started to suspect Ivor had, in the words of me dear old mum, "pulled a runner."

Even though, looking at it logically, an accident was the obvious explanation, the most *likely* explanation, when I did spot the smashed and splintered end of that guard rail, it seemed unreal.

"Go back," I told Jake. "Turn around and go back."

We had to drive on for a couple of miles before we could find a turnout. Jake hung a neat three-point turn, and we started down the road again.

"There." I pointed. He pulled as far to the side as he could, turned his hazards on, and we crossed the road.

There were no skid marks, which was why I'd nearly missed it the first time. The guard rail was one of those old wooden ones, and the very end had been clipped off—also making it easy to overlook. The scrub and shrubs around it had been ripped out of the ground, and there were deep tracks where tires had churned through the mud on their way over the edge.

The tracks had dried hard but were starting to soften in the rain pelting down from the huge cumulus clouds overhead.

"Jesus."

Rain? Those fat, sleety drops threatened to freeze into actual snow. There were still patches of snow from the last storm in the shade along the side of the road, and the silence was so profound it seemed to swallow all sound as we stood there.

Not all sound. I could hear the patter of rain, and the waterproof crinkle of our coats.

Snow and pine trees. Four days after Christmas it smelled more like Christmas than Christmas had.

I hoped whoever had gone over the edge had walked away, but that didn't seem likely.

Jake scanned the steep hillside with his binoculars.

"Do you see anything?"

He shook his head.

I ran my fingers over the bare, splintered edge of the guardrail. Impossible to know when that had happened, but it looked relatively fresh to me. If a car crashed through, the driver would only have a minute or two—slightly over a hundred yards of a muddy, grassy slope in—which to try and save himself. Then the shelf of grass and trees fell away in a much steeper drop. A hell of a way down, judging by the frozen clack and clatter of pebbles scattering down the hillside.

"There," Jake said suddenly. He unlooped his binoculars and handed them to me. "Nine o'clock. There's a glint of turquoise beneath those sugar pines."

I trained the binoculars in the direction he'd indicated and caught the glint of metallic blue beneath the branches. It was just about to the edge of the grassy slope. The tall pines had prevented the car from sliding off the shelf of rock and soil and plummeting to whatever lay below. "Got it."

Jake was already walking into the road, looking for landmarks as he tried to phone for help.

"He might have made it out," I said. "It's not that steep from down there to here. Or he might have been thrown out of the car too."

Or he could be sitting behind the steering wheel, dead for the past four days.

Jake swore. "I'm not getting enough signal."

I checked my phone. Shook my head.

He came to stand with me at the guard rail. "It might be an old wreck. I need to make sure it's not, before I drag emergency services up here. It's best if you stay up top to flag—"

"Save your strength for the climb," I interrupted. "You know as well as I do that you going down there on your own is a bad idea."

"I don't want you trying to make that climb." Flat and uncompromising.

It was sort of sweet, that innocent belief that he would deliver his commands and I would obey.

"I know you don't," I said. "And I don't want you trying to make that climb either. Although it's more of a hike than a climb. But we're both going. See, this is where all those god-awful breakfast smoothies and evening walks and other heart-healthy behaviors come in. There is no reason I can't hike down there. It's not that much of a trek, and I'm fully capable of making it—with or without you."

"Adrien, I'm not—"

"*Jake.*"

He shut up.

"You're not going to win this one, so quit wasting time." I walked around the end of the barrier and started down the slope.

I didn't look back, but I heard the crunch of his boots behind me. If it was possible to convey disapproval with footsteps, he was doing it.

In fairness, it was a tougher hike than it looked. And the patches of snow and ice made it more challenging still. But it was well within my capabilities, and definitely preferable to waiting at the top without a clue as to what was happening. The grass gave a dead, frozen bite beneath our boots. The sleety rain stung my skin.

The car, a turquoise blue Kia Forte, was situated roughly one hundred feet from the road.

Jake said, "It's his license plate."

Pretty unlikely it could be a *different* turquoise blue Kia Forte, but still my heart sank.

We could see from the tire tracks where it had jumped the berm, slammed down, and then slithered and fishtailed its way into a stand of tall sugar pines.

Studying those snaking grooves of tire tracks, I asked Jake, "Do you think he was still in control of the car?"

"No skid marks. So he either went over deliberately, or he fell asleep. I'm guessing he fell asleep."

As we reached the car, I saw through the broken glass that there was a figure slumped over the steering wheel.

"Shit," Jake muttered, moving past me.

My legs felt suddenly wobbly, and I had to steady myself on the nearest tree trunk.

What had I expected? A belated Christmas miracle? The minute we spotted the car, Ivor's fate was a foregone conclusion.

I leaned back against the tree and took a couple of bracing lungfuls of clean mountain air. Poor Kevin. How the hell were we going to tell him?

What a horrible end to the holidays. To the year. To a life.

Overhead, the wind made a ghostly sound through the tree branches.

Jake was still leaning in the car, checking for whatever he was checking. "Hey, Adrien," he said, and his voice sounded odd. "This guy's alive."

"*What?*"

He ducked out of the car and stared at me. His eyes were so bright they looked green. "I'm getting a pulse. Not much. But he's hanging on."

"For *four* days?"

Jake assented. "We've got to get him help."

"Yes. Right."

"We can't call out. One of us has to go."

I knew what he was saying. If somebody had to go, then somebody had to stay. And Jake, police academy trained, was the better driver and the person best equipped to get help fast.

"I'll stay."

I could see the relief in his eyes. And the worry.

He moved away from the car and rested his hands on my shoulders. "It's going to be at least an hour. Probably longer. He's circling the drain now. Understand?"

"Yes."

"I'm sorry to do this to you."

"Go," I said impatiently, because sympathy made it worse, and Ivor was the guy who deserved it, anyway. "I can handle this."

Jake squeezed my shoulders and took off at a jog up the slope. Not that I'd ever had a doubt who was in better shape, but…

After a moment, I braced for the worst and turned to look in the car. Good thing breakfast had been so long ago because the smell was unholy. Mostly it was blood. There was a *lot* more blood than I had expected. To add to the horror movie ambiance, a bone stuck out of Ivor's thigh.

I had to back away and gulp a couple more breaths of that pure mountain air. I took another look at Ivor. His face was a mass of dried blood and bruises, and he was covered in white powder, which I took at first to be snow, then realized it was from his air bag going off.

Footsteps pounded toward me. I straightened up, and Jake delivered an armload of stuff to me. A blanket, bottles of water, and a tan canvas bag which probably contained a first aid kit, and which I was not about to try and use. This guy had enough problems without me trying to play doctor.

Jake was breathing hard, but he locked a hand around my neck, kissed me, and without saying a word, sprinted off again.

Here was a salutary lesson about keeping emergency supplies in your car. My emergency supplies consisted of a sweatshirt, a flashlight, a bottle of Evian, and a four-year-old Kind bar. Granted, I'd never been a Boy Scout.

I shook the folds out of the blanket and tried to tuck it very carefully around Ivor. He never moved. In fact, I couldn't tell if he was still breathing. I picked up his hand, and it was cold. Granted, it *was* cold out.

I knelt down in the damp pine needles beside the open door, and still holding his hand, began to talk to him.

"Ivor? I don't know if you can hear me. And waking you up right now is probably not a good idea. But you've got to hang on. No matter how much it hurts. No matter how scared you are. People care about you. Kevin cares about you."

I fell silent at the sound of a car engine disappearing into the vast and windswept distance.

This poor bastard. To wind up with me at his deathbed? Jesus.

I'd had Jake.

That had been one heck of a consolation prize. It had also been the reason I'd decided to live.

I steadied myself, gave Ivor's icy hand another squeeze. Tried not to look at that bone sticking up a few inches from my face. "Listen to me, Ivor. You can do this. You're the only one who *can* do this. You can make it back. I've been in this same place. Well, it was actually the ocean, but same thing. Life-threatening injuries and everybody thinking you're dying. Don't do it. Don't let go. Come home. Come home to Kevin. He's waiting for you. Everything you want is on this side…"

I must have talked—babbled—for ninety minutes straight before help finally, finally arrived. When it did show up, it came in a fleet of trucks with screaming sirens. I could have cried with relief. Maybe I didn't really know Ivor, but I was starting to take his survival personally.

Jake was first across the grassy slope.

I so stiff by then, I could barely stand. Jake helped me to my feet and wrapped his arm around me.

"You okay?"

I nodded.

"Is he—"

"I don't know. I thought for a while he might be. But…I don't know."

We scrambled out of the way of the emergency services team, waiting and watching as the paramedics worked over Ivor for a few moments. Then one of them backed out of the wreckage and yelled, "We've got a pulse! He's alive!"

* * * * *

Within the hour Ivor was airlifted to a trauma center in Modesto.

Jake and I rendezvoused there with Kevin, and we all waited to hear whether Ivor would survive. The injuries sustained in the crash, though serious, were not life-threatening in themselves, but exposure, dehydration, and shock had left him in critical and unstable condition.

Kevin was in rough shape, and it just wasn't in me to leave him to face that wait alone.

"Hell, yeah, we'll wait with him," Jake said when stepped out to get coffee.

By the end of day on Thursday, the entire Arbuckle clan had flown into Modesto to gather at Ivor's bedside, and while relations with Kevin were not cordial, no one tried to get him to leave or seemed to believe he didn't have a right to be there. A truce seemed to have been struck. At least during the interim of waiting to hear whether Ivor would live or die.

The Arbuckles paid Jake for his services. One thing in their favor: they were not cheap. They granted him a bonus on top of his regular fee, recognizing that he had gone the extra mile. In fact, he had gone the extra three hundred and forty-two miles.

Mrs. Arbuckle asked me to send her regards to Lisa. Terrill pretended we had never been properly introduced.

So that was Thursday.

Which pretty much also described Friday—and Friday night. In between giving Kevin pep talks, I spoke to Natalie, who was phoning me with regular and slightly alarming updates from Cloak and Dagger. As predicted, Warren believed she should get rid of the baby ASAP. Angus believed they should get married immediately, even if the baby didn't turn out to be his.

"Please don't rush into making any decisions," I pleaded. "There's plenty of time to figure this out."

To my astonishment, she agreed. "I know. I have to think for two now."

"Well, yes. That's right."

"Which reminds me. When you get back down here, can you pick up some more of those Laceys cookies? They're the only thing I can eat right now."

"Yes. I can do that."

"When are you coming back? Do I have to spend another weekend doggy-watching? Should I leave Mr. Tomkins at the store or do I bring him home to Porter Ranch?"

"It depends on what happens up here. I'm hoping we'll know by this evening."

"He misses you. Mr. Tomkins, I mean. He's started sleeping on your desk."

"Just like me."

She giggled, which was kind of a relief. To hear someone laugh again.

Angus also phoned. He was not laughing. He wanted me to convince Natalie that they needed to get married as soon as possible.

"Look, you didn't think your relationship was any of my business before, so don't try to drag me into it now," I replied. "This is between you and Natalie. Besides which, you don't even know if this baby is yours."

"I don't care. I still want to marry her. I told you I loved her."

I sighed. "I repeat, that's between you and Nat. I don't believe rushing into anything is a good idea though."

Lisa also had a choice thing or two to say about the den of iniquity disguised as a bookstore I was running.

"You're the one who insisted she come and work for me," I reminded her. "Anyway, it's even odds that rock band reject Warren knocked her up. My money's on him."

"Please don't use the phrase 'knocked up' when speaking of your sister."

"Just saying. I'm running a bookstore, not a dating service. Everybody involved in this is a consenting adult. Well, except the baby. Poor little germ."

Emma, who I managed to FaceTime with while *Famille Dauten* waited for their connecting flight in Amsterdam, was the one person who was unreservedly joyful about Natalie's pregnancy. She was thrilled at the idea of being an aunt and busily picking out baby names. The top contenders appeared to be Boris for a boy baby and Scout for a girl.

"That's going to be really confusing if she's got the same name as my dog," I objected.

Emma was unmoved. She pointed out that they would probably not share a birthday, and therefore there would be no problem with conflicting birthday cakes.

I know when I'm beaten.

Toward dawn on Saturday, Kevin got the news that the doctors believed Ivor had turned the corner. He had regained consciousness and was asking for Kevin.

While the hospital staff remained guardedly optimistic, Kevin was jubilant.

"He was coming home," Kevin told us after the bedside reunion. "He wanted to spend Christmas together. He said spending that time with his family clarified his feelings. He wanted to be with me." Kevin's eyes were wet. "I know we're going to be okay."

Hopefully. Ivor had some pretty serious injuries and a long road to recovery, but having the right person at your side could make all the difference.

I glanced at Jake and found he was studying me with a thoughtful expression. I smiled and he smiled, but I could tell something was on his mind.

It took me awhile to remember what that something might be.

"You know, we weren't so far from Pine Shadow," Jake said after we'd made our good-byes and headed for the freeway.

"I know. It would have been nice to spend some time up there again."

He glanced at me. "It's not too late. We could turn around and head back. We could celebrate New Year's at the ranch and spend a nice, quiet weekend up there."

Yes. Perfect. The perfect way to start the New Year. In the place where I had first acknowledged that I loved Jake. And had suspected he even cared for me too. A couple of days of peace and quiet. Just me and Jake and a healthy distance from everyone else's problems.

"I would love that. Let's make a plan and let's do it," I said. "But not tonight and not this weekend. We've got a New Year's Eve party to attend."

CHAPTER TWELVE

"**Y**ou know, you don't have to go," Jake said as we were dressing for his parents' New Year's Eve party.

It was the second time he'd said it, and I paused in knotting my tie. "Do you not want me to go?" I wasn't angry or hurt or anything other than concerned that this evening be what Jake needed it to be. Not like I was exactly looking forward to being the star attraction at the family freak show.

"Of course I want you there. But…we're Irish. We get drunk and say stupid things. I can't guarantee that someone there tonight won't say something stupid."

It was tempting to answer, "I'm English. We stay sober, kick ass, and enslave your lot for eight hundred years." That would not have reduced his stress level any. I finished knotting my tie, assessing the results.

The white and red candy cane tie—a gift from Lauren—made the Hugo Boss blazer and black jeans look less like I was going to a funeral.

"It's okay, Jake. I'm not going to have a heart attack if someone is rude to me. I work in retail, remember? Let's go into it with a positive attitude."

Jake laughed and shook his head. He came up behind me and nuzzled beneath my ear. "Okay, baby. And God help them."

* * * * *

Pa and Ma Riordan lived in Glendale, not too far from Jake's old place.

The house looked exactly as I'd imagined. Like June and Ward Cleaver still lived there. Maybe they did. Maybe that was the trouble.

No white picket fence, but it was a traditional 1950s ranch-style sitting on a half-acre lot with mature oak trees. There was a basketball hoop in the driveway and a tree house with a rope ladder in the backyard. Colored Christmas lights were wound through the trees and along the eaves of the house. Cars crowded the driveway and I could hear music from inside.

Jake didn't say a word as we strolled up the brick walk. I wanted to reassure him, but I didn't know if reassurance was called for—and I didn't know if it would be welcome in this situation.

So, yes, I was nervous. Something about the glimpse of that damned tree house had triggered a whole host of insecurities I'd figured I was over.

Jake ran the bell.

His dad answered the door. I knew him at once, because he looked like an older, heavier version of Jake—although it was hard to picture Jake going in for oversize cardigans and argyle socks.

He looked slightly taken aback. "James?" He shoved open the screen door. "Come in. Come in."

"Happy New Year." Jake handed over a bottle of Laphroaig. "This is Adrien. Adrien, this is my old man."

I said automatically, "Pleased to meet you, sir."

Even if Jake hadn't informed me years ago that his old man was a cop, I'd have known it instantly. He gave me a searching look from beneath startlingly black brows, shook hands, and instructed me to call him "James Senior."

Which, after all, is an improvement over *Officer.*

The house smelled of baking and cinnamon candles. We were ushered inside and down the long hallway lined with photos of Riordans old and new. Somehow my eye zeroed right onto Jake and Kate's wedding photo. Kate stared at me. I blinked first.

"Look who's here," Jake's dad called in warning, and a slim woman came bustling around the corner.

Jake's mom was a few years older than Lisa. Her hair was styled in a silver bob recalling TV moms of an earlier generation. Her face was youthful and still pretty. She wore what I think used to be called ski slacks and one of those deliberately ugly Christmas sweaters. On her, retro was kind of cute.

She hugged me briefly, told me to call her Janie, and ushered us into the middle of what appeared to be a cop convention in the living room.

Yeah, they were *all* cops. Clearly. In fact, I wouldn't have sworn that Jake's mom wasn't a retired desk sergeant. Father, brothers, wives, girlfriends... There were a couple of toddlers playing with toy police cars in front of the television.

I won't say that everyone stopped talking when we entered the room, but...yeah, for a couple of seconds everyone stopped talking. Janie began to make the introductions, and people put aside their drinks and got to their feet.

Neal, the middle brother, was a police detective with Glendale PD. He took after Janie's side of the family. Shorter, slimmer, browner. He was married to Brenna, who looked so much like Kate my heart skipped a couple of beats. Brenna was also a detective with Glendale PD. The two toddlers, Rory and Cory, belonged to them.

A great deal of explanation seemed to be going into the introductions, and I think it was because they had no idea what to say to us. Or certainly not to me. It was pretty obvious no one had thought we'd show up.

"Very nice to meet you," I said, shaking hands with Neal and Brenna and Dusty. Dusty was Danny's girlfriend. She had blue eyes, black hair, and adorable freckles. She worked Metro Traffic.

Danny, Jake's youngest brother, looked like a shorter, squarer version of Jake. He had not yet made detective at Pasadena PD, but was naturally working toward that ultimate life's goal. One thing Jake had told me was that Danny was having a particularly tough time with Jake's revelation, and his handshake was hard and hasty. He did not wipe his fingers afterwards, but I think it went through his mind.

In fairness, his palm was moist. I think he was genuinely nervous.

"Danny." Jake's hand rested lightly on my back.

"James." Danny did not meet his eyes.

Janie came to the rescue asking us about our Christmas.

It occurred to me that I had made little to no effort to learn anything about Jake's family. My relationship with him had existed outside the boundaries of his normal life for so long that even once we were officially a couple I had stuck to the old parameters. So in that sense, we were all starting from go. My only advantage was I'd known they existed.

They were a boisterous bunch—everyone, including the kids, talked at the same time. And talked loudly. But then, they were well-lubricated by the time we'd shown up.

The subject of Jake's trip to London—the idea of Jake traveling to foreign lands—was a source of great interest and greater amusement.

Listening to them, I realized how absolutely alien my own family must seem to Jake—and what a really patient guy he could be.

"What would you like to drink, Adrien?" Janie touched my arm tentatively.

"Anything really. Beer. Wine. Whatever you have." I smiled at her, and she blinked.

"You know, you look so much like that actor. I forget his name now."

"Montgomery Clift?"

"Who? Oh no. No. Matt Somebody. He used to play a jewel thief, I think."

"I'll get him a drink, Mom," Brenna said, joining us. She gave me a cool smile and nodded for me to follow her into the kitchen.

Having had sisters for a while, I knew what that look meant. I braced for trouble.

Breanna went straight to the fridge, which was papered in childish colorings. I thought some of the crayon drawings looked like early attempts at mug shots, but maybe I was wrong.

"What would you like?" Breanna was brisk. "Beer? We have everything."

Not the fixings for Black Orchids, I bet. I said, "Maybe a wine cooler?"

"I can do you a wine spritzer."

"Sure."

She scooped a clear plastic cup into a giant bag of ice in the sink and said, "Kate's more than my sister-in-law. She's my best friend."

Fair enough.

I said, "This is hard for everybody."

"Yes. It is."

"I'll try not to make it harder."

She splashed some ginger ale and wine into the cup and handed it to me. Her green gaze held mine steadily. "It's just…going to take some of us longer than others."

I nodded.

Her smile was more of a grimace. She walked out of the kitchen. I sipped my drink, examined the drawings on the fridge, and then followed her out. Jake was watching for me, and I smiled.

He looked relieved. I came to stand beside him while he continued to argue good-naturedly with Neal about something only a cop or an ex-cop would care about. I liked Neal, though. He made eye contact, and he tried to address comments my way now and then.

The TV was on with the sound muted. *New Year's Eve Live* with Anderson Cooper and Special Co-Host Kathy Griffin silently counted down from Times Square. Meanwhile a stereo system was playing an endless loop of Peggy Lee, mostly holiday hits, but every now and then "Is That All There Is?" popped up.

Each time, Jake would look at me and we'd smile at each other.

Janie told me all about Cory and Rory, which took longer than one might imagine, considering they were only four years old. I told her my sister was expecting and we were all pretty excited, which was certainly true. Although agitated might have been more accurate.

I ate Chex Mix and chicken wings and Swedish meatballs and onion dip and celery sticks filled with blue-cheese spread. I had two ginger ale wine spritzers, and then I settled down to drinking straight ginger ale, having offered to be the designated driver that night. I figured Jake was going to need the numbing effect of alcohol more than me, but he was not drinking much as far as I could tell.

"What is it you do?" Dusty asked me when we happened to meet over the dips and veggies.

"I own a bookstore."

"I didn't think Jake liked to read that much."

So many responses available to me. I settled for, "Well. You know."

They did not, of course. It was quite obvious they had no clue.

Which had probably been a lot of the problem. The other problem was they had known and loved Kate, and even if I'd been another woman, I would not have been welcome. They were trying. I could see that. For Jake's sake they were going to make the effort.

And I would do the same.

"You like Peggy Lee?" Jake's dad asked in a challenging tone when he found me studying the photos in the entry hall.

"I do, actually."

He looked nonplussed. "What songs do you like?"

"For starters, I like this one. 'My Dear Acquaintance.'"

"What do you know,"—he called over his shoulder—"someone else in this house has good taste!"

There were immediate cheers and boos from the living room, and James Senior chuckled, looking pleased with himself.

I've had better times at New Year's Eve parties. I won't argue that. It was a long-ass evening, and we'd had a long-ass couple of days preceding it, but as the evening stretched on and on and Anderson Cooper and Kathy Griffin—who Jake's mom kept calling Kathy Lee—looked colder and more strained, Jake's family began to defrost. Began to warm up. And as Jake stopped looking so pinched and on guard, my heart began to warm too.

Maybe it was the booze. They could drink, that was for sure. Even Janie could put it away. Whatever it was, round about eleven thirty, the brothers started slapping Jake on the back during the storytelling, and the sister-in-law and aspiring sister-in-law stopped visibly wincing every time they caught my eye.

By the time the ball dropped—Pacific Coast Time replay—and we all gathered around to sing "Auld Lang Syne," I felt like maybe, with enough time and effort from both sides, *maybe* it really would be okay.

When the song ended and everyone turned to kiss their spouse, Jake rested his hand against my face. His own face was flushed and his eyes were bright. He looked self-conscious in a way he had not looked all evening. I opened my mouth to say—I have no idea what. *Hey, don't worry about it.*

Old habits die hard.

But he cut me off with a kiss, his mouth firm, almost gentle on my own.

Come to think of it, it was the best New Year's Eve party ever.

* * * * *

"I mean, if you can put up with my family," I said, continuing our conversation from the drive home. I spat toothpaste into the sink and turned on the taps.

Jake replied, but I couldn't hear over the rush of water.

"What?"

My gaze fell on Tomkins, who was delicately perched on the rim of the toilet bowl. "If you do, I'm flushing you down," I informed him. "You're not licking me with toilet water tongue."

"I hope you're talking to the cat," Jake called.

I rinsed, used the towel, and poked my head out of the bathroom. "What?"

"My mother said you have very nice manners."

"I do."

"Yes. You do."

I stepped over Scout, who was observing events unfold in the bathroom like he was watching a play, and crossed the room to the bed. "And I'll keep having nice manners. Whatever we have to do to make this work."

Hopefully that didn't sound too inspirational posterish. *Teamwork! Change! Endurance!* Jake was watching me attentively. Very attentively for someone not already between the sheets.

He had discarded his jacket, loosened his tie, and removed his shoes, but that seemed to be as far as the disrobing had gone.

I said, "It's a great note to start the year on, I think. The fact that they invited us. Me, I mean. They wanted you there. That was obvious."

"Thank you for tonight."

"You don't have to thank me. I mean it. Your family is my family."

Unless they hurt him again, in which case next holiday season I'd be poisoning the gift baskets.

He was still giving me that look. I glanced around uncertainly—and did a double take. He had the gas fireplace blazing and a bottle of champagne uncorked and ready to go on the small table. Two flute glasses stood at the ready.

Like the night hadn't been long enough for him?

"Oh, you found the champagne glasses. Great! Now if we can just find the flannel sheets..."

Jake drew a deep breath. "You know the other night when you were talking about being a better boyfriend?"

"Okay," I said quickly. "I haven't signed the dog up for obedience classes yet, but I *did* talk to Natalie about not working every Sunday. I'll take three Sundays a month off so that she can have a Sunday too. And we're starting interviews next week."

He said quietly, seriously, as if I hadn't spoken, "Boyfriends don't come any better than you."

"*Oh*. Well..." I grinned. "Thanks. Of course you haven't really had many boyfriends to compare. Me and that homicidal maniac you used to go out with."

He said—and he was not smiling, not seeing the humor—"That homicidal maniac was never my boyfriend."

"Okay. Sorry."

The clock downstairs struck two. We listened to the silvery chime die away. It sounded...portentous. Not that two was an especially significant number.

Well, come to think of it, yes. Two *was* a significant number. Especially for us.

I said, "It's the first day of the first New Year we've spent together. Shall we drink to it?"

"Yes. first…" Jake's voice got that funny, slightly winded sound to it again. "I have one last Christmas present for you."

"Oh? Really? You don't want to save it until next year?"

"No." He looked momentarily confused. "I don't."

"Okay." I can't pretend that I wasn't starting to feel anxious at the strange way he was acting. Even the dog seemed to sense something was up, turning his head this way and that, like he couldn't quite catch the frequency. Tomkins stuck his head out of the bathroom, whiskers twitching.

Jake inclined his head toward the table. I followed his gaze and noticed there was a small white-wrapped box tied with a gold silk bow next to the ice bucket.

My heart gave a stutter as it hadn't done in six months.

"This is it? This is for me?" Now *my* voice sounded funny.

Jake nodded.

I picked up the box and gave the ribbon a tug; it fell away with a silky whisper.

Jake said suddenly, as though he couldn't take the suspense, "I brought it with us to London, but it didn't seem like the right time. I hope this is."

I unpeeled the paper and studied the small blue velvet box. I looked at him and swallowed.

"Jake."

He said, and his voice cracked ever so slightly, "I got this wrong the last time. I'm sorry. For that. And for—"

I said, "You think I don't know? You think there's some part of me that hasn't forgiven you?"

"No. But I understand if you're not ready yet to take a chance on… this."

"Jake. Come on." I opened the box and saw the gold, milgrain-edged band before it dissolved in the sudden, hot blur in my eyes.

I wiped my eyes, looked at him. In the soft light his gaze was shiny and solemn, his face a little pale.

"Will you marry me, Adrien-with-an-e?"

I closed my fingers around the loosened loop of his tie, drawing him slowly, inexorably in. Before our lips met, I whispered, "Baby, I thought you'd never ask."

ODDS AND SODS

THE ADRIEN ENGLISH MYSTERIES

AN INTERVIEW WITH ADRIEN ENGLISH

He is very drunk.

Preoccupied, tired, maybe a little lonely, he has let me refill his glass — ply him with liquor — in a way he ordinarily would not. It's not good for him, for one thing — not with that tricky heart of his. And he knows he has a tendency to…rock himself in the waters. So he's generally careful.

He's generally careful about most things, and yet…yet he keeps getting involved in murder. And with the wrong men.

You can tell a lot about a guy when he drinks. Adrien English is not a sloppy drunk. In fact, he gets more careful. Very serious — owlish, even. But his dark hair falls untidily into his blue eyes, and he has this little trick of watching me from under his lashes. He's not *flirting*, exactly…

He's better looking than I expected. Better looking than he thinks — a lot better looking than he thinks. And yet it's hard to put my finger on what it is. The eyes are lovely, of course. Nice nose. Stubborn chin. Mouth is a little too sensitive. Maybe it's just the trick of good bone structure. He needs a haircut but his hands are clean, well-cared for.

No ring.

I start with that.

"How are things going with Guy? You're still seeing him, right?"

He cocks a brow. I think he imagines it makes him look sardonic, but somehow it emphasizes the fact that his collar is undone one button too far, and his hair keeps falling in his eyes.

"Have you been talking to my mother?" he asks — he's amused. Mostly.

"No. I just know at the end of *The Hell You Say* things were moving in that direction."

"Ah." He sips his fifth Italian margarita. "Things are good. Guy is… good."

It's my turn to raise an eyebrow. "What about all that occult stuff he's into?"

He levels a long blue look at me and offers a kind of smirk. "Five fold kiss," he says succinctly.

I have no idea what he's talking about.

"So you're happy?"

"Of course." There must be something in his drink, the way he's staring into those amber depths. "Everything is great. Everything is… going very well. We're expanding the bookstore. And I just sold the film rights to my first book to Paul Kane's production company." He rubs his forehead — yes, he's going to have one hell of a headache tomorrow morning. "Everything's coming together. Natalie is working at Cloak and Dagger –"

I interrupt what is beginning to sound like rambling. "Do you ever hear from Angus?"

"Not so far…"

"How are you adjusting to Lisa's remarriage? Do you like being part of a big family?"

"Oh my God!" he says, and that's the first absolutely unguarded response he's given. "Oh. My. *God.*" He raises his head and stares at me like…words fail him.

"It's not going well?" Now that I didn't expect. "But they all like you. They care –"

"Believe me," he says. "I *know.*"

I have to bite my lip to keep a straight face. "Well, I think they're good for you."

He just gives me a long, dark long.

"I think you need more people in your life," I insist. "Maybe even a cat."

"A *cat?*"

"Every bookstore needs a cat."

He rolls his eyes, and now he's ignoring me. I study his profile. Yes, that is one stubborn chin.

You can tell guys who've grown up with money. Even though he's just wearing Levis and a simple white tailored shirt, he has this...air. It's more than grooming. It's more than the well-worn Bruno Magli loafers or the Omega watch. I don't think he realizes how much he's been pampered, protected — not really.

"What is it about you that seems to attract murder and violence?" I ask.

"Me?" Now I have his full astonished attention. "If you'll notice –" he's enunciating very carefully "I haven't been involved in a murder since — in nearly two years. Coincidence? I think not."

"You don't think you're bad luck or suffering from Jessica Fletcher Syndrome or something like that?"

He's giving me a hard, un-Adrien stare. "Why don't you ask me what you really came here to ask me?" he says quietly.

It's my turn to look away. When I glance back, he's still watching me — I'm apparently having more trouble with this than he is.

"All right. Did you read my interview with Jake Riordan?"

His mouth twists. "Yeah. So?"

"What do you think?"

"What is there to think?"

"Do you think Jake's happy with the choices he's made?"

"How the hell should I know?"

"Are you happy with the choices he's made?"

He opens his mouth, then closes it. Gives me a wry smile. All at once he seems a lot more sober. "He had to make the choices that were right for him, and I'm all right with that."

"Do you think if Jake came out, you could forgive him?"

"There's nothing to forgive."

"Do you think if Jake came out, you could have a future together?"

He says flatly, "That will never happen. Jake will never come out."

"But if he did –"

Impatiently, he says, "I don't want to talk theoretical bullshit. He won't. He can't. It's moot. There's no point talking about it. There's no point thinking about it."

"All right, already."

He grimaces, tosses off the rest of his margarita.

"Do you still love Jake?" I ask softly.

"No." He doesn't hesitate, he meets my eyes. He shakes his head.

"But you did? Once?"

His smile is a little bitter as he rises not quite steadily from the table. "Probably," he says. "It was a long time ago."

AN INTERVIEW WITH JAKE RIORDAN

It's eleven minutes after the hour when LAPD Homicide Detective Jake Riordan walks in. He moves with that alert but easy confidence I remember. He spots me immediately, joins me at the bar. He nods a curt hello, leans across to order a drink — what is that scent he wears? Soap, the leather of his jacket, a hint of his own clean sweat. He settles back on the stool and studies me. His eyes are hazel. I'd forgotten that — forgotten how long his eyelashes are too. I guess I didn't want to remember how attractive he is, but now that he's here in front of me...he's not easy to dismiss.

"Okay, Josh," he says, and that wry suggestion of a smile is sort of disarming. "What the hell is so important that it couldn't wait?"

"I need to ask you a couple of questions. And I need you to be straight with me."

"I'm always straight." He's not smiling.

"Listen, pal, your continued existence depends on the next five minutes."

He meets my gaze levelly. Lifts a broad shoulder. "Shoot."

"You'd be surprised at the number of people who want me to do just that."

His lifts his brows, apparently unimpressed. He dumps the shot in his beer. Picks the glass up and takes a sip. "It's always a possibility in my line," he says.

"I know." Oddly enough, he looks a little sympathetic, meeting my gaze. "You're married now," I say. "How's that going?"

His face closes. After a moment he says, "You know Kate lost the baby, right?"

"Yeah."

"Yeah. Well…" He sighs. "It's been rough. Rough on Kate. You know women. She keeps going over it. Thinking maybe it was something she did or didn't do."

"I'm not that interested in Kate. I want to know how you feel."

His expression is pained. "Jesus, Josh. How the hell do you think I feel? I wanted the kid. I wanted…" He stops. "Anyway. It's okay. It's good. I got what I wanted. She's a great girl." He corrects himself. "Woman."

"You used to do the clubs. Are you still active in the S/M scene?"

He gives me a long look. "You know damn well, I am, so why are you asking?"

"Not exactly *Leave it to Beaver* this marriage, is it?"

"No." He looks pointedly at his expensive wristwatch — the one Kate gave him for his birthday. "Next question."

"You were involved in a homosexual relationship for a while with Adrien English, a gay bookseller –" I hesitate as I note the fleeting softening of his expression. "That relationship ended in violence –"

"Violence." He shakes his head. "Jesus. I shoved him, he fell. I shouldn't have — I feel like hell every time I think of it, okay? I wouldn't — it was an extreme situation, and, yeah, I was jealous, frustrated, bitter, I admit it. All of it. I regret it." He gives me a level look. "Ask Adrien if he thinks I'd ever — never mind."

"Do you ever see Adrien anymore?"

"I tried calling him a couple of times. Left a message." He sips his drink. "He could get in touch if he wanted to."

"You're married!"

"I mean as friends! Jesus. You people. You know, guys can occasionally be close without jumping into the sack."

"You really *are* pretty damned insensitive," I say disgustedly. "No wonder Adrien wouldn't pick up the phone."

He finishes his drink. "That it?"

I study him for a long moment. "One last question. Do you still love Adrien?"

His hazel eyes meet mine, and just for a moment I see something — or maybe I want to see it. His face...changes. Just for a moment there's something almost too painful to look at. He doesn't answer, and I realize he *can't*. He recovers so fast I think I probably imagined it.

Jake gets up to leave. Without looking at me, he says, "Tell Adrien... tell him to take care of himself."

THE DARK TIDE PLAYLIST

Once upon a time, as a special treat, Josh created a special iTunes iMix playlist of the music that inspired the writing of *The Dark Tide*. You could go to iTunes and check it out, and even buy it if you wanted.

Unfortunately, Apple discontinued that feature a while ago. But here's the playlist.

Everytime We Say Goodbye – Sarah Vaughan

Chocolate – Snow Patrol

I Miss You – Incubus

Collide – Howie Day

This Is It – Staind

Strangers in a Car – Marc Cohn

Does This Mean You're Moving On? – The Airborne Toxic Event

Rain – Patty Griffin

Run – Snow Patrol

Bargain – The Who

At Last – Etta James

SLIPPERY WHEN WET: A VISIT WITH ADRIEN ENGLISH

He's swimming when we pull up in the driveway.

Through the ornate iron fence we can see the pool in the little tiled courtyard ringed by rose bushes. The roses look tattered in the bright July sunlight. No one is living at the house now--the house he grew up in--and the gardeners are not quite as conscientious as they were when Lisa was there to critique their performance. We can just make out the flash of a brown arm, brown shoulders, the top of his dark head as he cuts through the sparkling water. He's been swimming there nearly every day since his doctor pronounced him fit enough following his heart surgery. Swimming on his own--and I can see Jake tensing. His profile looks like stone. "Don't start in on him about swimming by

himself," I warn. "That's not going to go over well."

The words are so terse he nearly has to pry them out. "For a smart guy he makes a lot of dumb choices."

"Yeah, well I wouldn't bring that topic up either, if I were you."

The hazel eyes--surprisingly long-lashed—meet mine. "Whose side are you on?"

"I'm not on anyone's side."

"Uh huh."

He opens the car door and I follow him into the pool courtyard. Adrien has just completed a neat little flip turn off the far wall of the deep end and is swimming back toward us in smooth, long strokes. He hasn't seen us yet, didn't hear the clang of the gate closing after us. I can feel Jake's tension as he moves away from me, going to the edge of the pool.

Something alerts Adrien. He raises his face

from the water to snatch a breath of air, catches sight of us, and stops swimming.

He and Jake stare at each other across the choppy blue expanse of pool, and then he swims on to the shallow end. He walks up the stairs, catches the towel Jake tosses him. He holds it the folds in front of his chest; not pretty, the scars open heart surgery leaves. He turns his back, rubs down briskly, still not saying anything, and reaches for the shirt hanging on the back of the nearby chair, shrugs into it.

Jake is also not saying anything--but he watches Adrien with a hungry intensity.

When Adrien turns around, though, his face gives nothing away. It's an expression perfected from years of negotiating boring or trying social occasions staged by Lisa. He's smiling and appears relaxed, although those blue eyes- -as blue as the deep, shadowy end of the pool-- are wary.

"I wasn't expecting you," he says, and he sounds friendly enough.

"Not my idea," Jake says curtly.

I see acknowledgment of that flicker in Adrien's eyes. But maybe things have changed because Jake sees it too. He says, "I promised to give you time and I'm doing that." He nods at me. "But Lanyon has some questions for you."

"Not again." Just for an instant their glances meet and hold in perfect, amused understanding.

"It won't take that long," I assure them.

"You always say that," Adrien says.

"Yes, and I'm usually right, aren't I?"

"No comment." That's Jake.

I move over to the table beneath the flowered umbrella. Adrien's watch and some vials of heart meds are sitting there. That reminds me that there are still some things I need to check on. I pull out a chair and Jake pulls out a chair for Adrien who throws me a slightly bemused look and sits down. Jake pulls another chair, metal scraping cement. He angles it so that he's looking out over the pool--and can watch Adrien without his own expression giving him away.

"Okay," I say. "We may as well just get down to it. Now that Jake has come out, where do you see the relationship going?"

They both seem to freeze. "You don't have to answer that," Jake says to Adrien.

Adrien continues to stare at me as though Jake hasn't spoken. He says at last, "Well, that's the question, isn't it?"

"Er, yes."

"The answer is...I don't know."

Jake's profile hardens minutely. He still doesn't say anything.

Adrien throws him a quick look. "I'm glad Jake came out. For his sake." He reaches his hand and Jake takes it immediately. They study each other over their clasped hands and there is such affection there. But maybe that's all that's all there is at this point? Not that that friendship wouldn't mean a lot--for both of them.

Slowly, carefully--he obviously does not wish to inflict pain--Adrien says, "I don't know if this will even make sense. For most of my adult life I thought I was...going to die young. My dad had a bad heart and he died when he was younger than I am now. I just accepted it and lived my life the best I could. But one side of that was...I didn't really think about some of the choices I made because I didn't ever think

I'd have to live with them that long."

He's smiling a funny sort of smile. Jake has turned his face so that I can't see his expression at all, but I see his throat move.

"But now, supposedly, I'm going to be pretty much okay. I mean... within limits, obviously. And it's...just...weird. Suddenly I'm not sure..."

I see Jake squeeze his hand, lightly, almost reassuringly, and then free his own.

"Okay, well let's leave that for now," I say quickly. "Let's go back a bit. Remember ClaudeLa Pierra?"

"Of course," Adrien says. "I was thinking about him the other day. I had a dream about him when I was in the hospital. That he came to visit me and brought me chicken soup. I still miss him."

"What about Robert Hersey?"

"Yeah," he says softly. "I won't forget Rob."

Jake moves restively. "Is there a point to this-- besides depressing him?"

Adrien shoots him a look that seems equal parts exasperation and affection. "I'm not depressed. I don't want to forget either of them. They were both a big part of my life. Rob in particular."

"Okay, here's a question for Jake. What did you feel after you had broken things off with Adrien and you sat outside Cloak and Dagger Books and saw that he was with Guy?"

No hesitation. "I thought I'd made the biggest fucking mistake of my life."

Adrien clenches his jaw and looks away.

"Will you keep in touch with Guy?" I ask him.

"Of course!" He sounds startled, his eyes returning to mine.

That's right, I remember. He stays friends with his exes.

"Is Angus coming back to the store?"

"No," says Jake very definitely.

Adrien raises his eyebrows. "I get a postcard from him now and again. We'll see."

"Are you going to keep the cat?"

"What cat?" asks Jake.

"Would you like a cat?" Adrien inquires of him.

"You have a cat?"

"No."

"Yes," I say.

Jake says, "I thought you always wanted a dog?"

"I do want a dog. I mean, if I lived in a place where I could have a dog. Which I don't."

"Well, speaking of that, say you two did move in together. What would you get for housewarming gifts and from whom?"Adrien blinks.

Jake says, "That's pretty much theoretical. Why don't you just ask the one about two cars starting off at the same point on a straight road facing opposite directions?"

Adrien laughs.

"What do you two think of each other's taste in music?"

"Hey," Adrien says, "are you going to do us one of those play list thingies like you did the last time?"

"Maybe. You didn't answer the question. Do you two have a song?"

They exchange looks. "Do we have a song?" Adrien asks.

Jake looks blank.

"What about couples counseling? Did you ever think of that?"

"We're not a couple," Jake says before Adrien can.

"If you were a couple, how do you think your families would take the news?"

Jake says nothing. Adrien bites his lip. I can't tell if he's trying not to laugh or is truly embarrassed.

"I think it would take everybody some getting used to," he says diplomatically.

Jake snorts.

"If you were a couple, do you think you'd live together?"

"We're not a couple," Adrien points out shortly.

"True. Well, maybe you could just live together as friends. Like... um, the Odd Couple. Jake's a pretty good cook, you know," I tell Adrien.

"And you don't look you've gained much weight since your surgery."

"I have to eat the right things. Watch my cholesterol now."

"Well, maybe you should figure out what those things are so you could eat some of them," Jake says.

"Funny."

"You know, those Lean Cuisines are high in sodium. So's Tab."

Adrien says to me, "Look what you started."

"Sorry. Different question. What will you do if Murder, He Mimed is optioned for a screenplay?"

"Move to France." He adds coolly, "I may move to France anyway."

Jake gives him a long, narrow look which he meets straight on.

"Okaaay, Jake, maybe we should talk a little about your relationship with Paul."

"Yes," Adrien purrs. "Let's talk about that."

"There's nothing to talk about. It was sex."

Both Adrien and I start to respond to that, but Adrien stops himself and says brusquely, "Anyway, ancient history."

Jake, watching him, opens his mouth, then closes it again. "If you want to know something, ask." His tone isn't gentle, exactly, but it isn't as harsh as I'd expect.

"Not my business," Adrien says curtly.

Uh oh. Not good. I go for a neutral topic.

"Will you go for another vacation at Pine Shadow ranch?

"I don't know," he says wearily. "There are a lot of memories..." He reaches for his watch and checks the time.

Jake meets my eyes. I begin to perceive the real problem here might actually be Adrien. I guess that would be a pleasant change.

Or not.

"Jake," I say, "do you think you'll ever forgive yourself for almost getting Adrien killed?

"No." He sounds almost cordial. "Do you?"

"Uh..."

Adrien says impatiently, "Nothing that happened in that damned book--or this fucking series--was Jake's fault. I made my own choices and I knew what the risks were going in."

"You do take a lot of risks."

"Great. Now I'm being psychoanalyzed. Okay, you want the truth. I guess maybe I did push things sometimes. I know it's going to sound weird, but I always felt a little...invulnerable. I know that doesn't make sense given the fact that my health has never been the greatest, but dying isn't--wasn't--something that ever scared me. At least...I didn't want to die violently or painfully, but quick always sounded pretty good to me."

Jake is listening to this with great attention.

Adrien draws a deep breath. "So that's changed and it's one of the things that scares me sort of. For the first time I feel like...I feel...I don't know. Like I need to be very careful." His voice sounds a little choky, but he pushes past it. "So don't give Jake a hard time over my own bad decisions."

"Okay." Given the look on Jake's face I figure he'll give himself enough of a hard time without my input.

Jake is staring at the pool like he's searching for sea monsters. Adrien's head is tipped back and he's staring up at the white clouds. His drying hair is starting to wave. It's longer than he usually wears it.

"Next question. Jake, how do you think you're going to be able to keep Adrien from assisting in your PI cases? Especially if you make an office in the newly remodeled book bookstore?"

"W-w-what?" That's from Adrien.

Jake asks alertly, "What makes you think I'm going to have an office in the bookstore?"

"Well, it's a pretty big building. It used to be an old hotel, right? And Adrien isn't going to be using all of it. Plus...you don't have an office right now, do you?"

"No." He looks uncomfortable. "I'm using an answering machine and meeting clients at a coffee house."

"Getting a lot of clients?"

He's avoiding looking at Adrien who is watching him with a little frown. "Not a lot. Yet."

"So how would you keep Adrien from getting involved in your cases?"

"I'm not getting involved in any more cases."

Adrien absently rubs his chest. Jake's eyes narrow, watching him.

I try another tack, reading from my notebook, "Adrien, you once expressed that Jake was your 'equal' which allowed you to truly get what you wanted without holding back. Supposing that, recognizing a person as your equal happens very quickly and early on in relationship, what qualities of Jake did you perceive in making this decision?"

I can see him thinking this over. "He's not afraid of me," he says astonishingly.

"Are guys generally afraid of you?"

He's still thinking how he wants to phrase this.

"Not exactly. I mean, my health was never an issue for him, for one thing. That meant a lot to me." That's for Jake, and Jake tips his head curtly in acceptance. "But also...he didn't find the fact that I had a brain or a sense of humor off-putting. He likes who I am. Who I really am, and who I really am is a lot harder and a lot tougher than a lot of people realize. That never scared him."

He looks at Jake for confirmation. Jake nods.

"I never had to pull my punches with him," Adrien says. "Or him with me."

"Yeah, well speaking of punches. How about that famous shove that he gave you in The Hell You Say."

"Oh my fucking God not that again." That's from Adrien. Jake draws a deep breath and says nothing. "Look, if I don't have a problem with it--"

"You've got a bad heart and he shoved you down."

"First off, he shoved me, but the fact that I fell was a fluke. He didn't punch me. He didn't kick me. He didn't keep hitting me. He shoved me. And I've shoved him other times. That's what I mean. He treated me like I treated him.

Like I was normal."

"Jake, do you have anything to say for yourself?"

"I'm not making excuses for it. There isn't any."

"Why do you think it happened?"

"Oh, come on!" Adrien says, furiously. "It's obvious why."

"Jake?"

"What, are you supposed to be the fucking marriage counselor?"

Jake puts a hand on his shoulder. "Just calm down." For an instant his eyes are almost tender.

To me he says, "You've asked me this before, and I've gone over that shove in my mind again and again. I didn't mean to knock him down. I felt sick when he hit the floor. When I saw his face."

His keeps his own face stern by effort. "There isn't an excuse, but the explanation is...everything was closing in on me. I know it was my own choice, my own decision, but I felt trapped with it, and then I saw--saw as clear as daylight-- what was going to happen with him and Captain Crunch. It was right there and I had let it happen."

"I don't want to talk about this again," Adrien says tightly.

"Is Adrien your equal?" I ask Jake.

His grin is wry. "Oh yeah. In every way that counts he's the strongest guy I know."

I glance over my notes. I can see Adrien is not going to sit still for much longer, and Jake is clearly hoping to grab a private word with him.

"Adrien, are you tired of being loved for your mind?"

"All this time I thought it was for my money."

"It is," Jake assures him.

"Jake, What do you really think of Lisa?"

"I plead the Fifth."

"Do you think Jake is capable of monogamy, and if you were together, would you expect that of him?"

Adrien automatically looks at Jake. "Yes, yes, and that's a very big if."

"Jake?"

"What he said."

"Okay, gentlemen." I flip shut my notebook.

"That's all I have. I expect the rest will be answered one way or the other in The Dark Tide.

That's your final adventure. Any last words before it begins?"

Adrien turns to Jake. His mouth curves in a reluctant smile. "See you on the other side."

"I'll be waiting," Jake says.

FLYING HIGH; THE ADRIEN ENGLISH AND JAKE RIORDAN CHRISTMAS INTERVIEW

It takes longer to locate them than I'd planned.

LAX is always busy and four days before Christmas it's a madhouse straight out of Dickens. People arriving. People departing. So many people. I see security guards arguing with holiday travelers armed with poinsettias and gaily wrapped parcels never designed to fit into overhead bins. Overhead, the fuzzy holiday music is interrupted for nearly unintelligible announcements of delayed flights and requests for missing passengers.

At last I track them down to Terminal 7 and Wolfgang Puck Express. For a moment I hang back, observing them.

They're sharing a margherita pizza and a couple of Sam Adams. There is also a Caesar salad but neither of them is paying it any attention.

As a matter of fact, they're neither of them paying much attention to anything but the other. Their casual body language mirrors each other, their gazes rest on each other's faces as they talk.

Jake wears black jeans and a black shirt. His hair is a fraction longer and he's put on a little weight since the summer. He looks healthy and relaxed. He hasn't lost the old, instinctive alertness, though he hasn't spotted me yet.

Adrien is wearing jeans and a cashmere sweater over a white tee. The blue of the sweater picks up the blue of his eyes even from this distance. It doesn't look like he's put on weight but he's lost that tired, fine-drawn look.

As I near their table, Adrien nudges Jake's foot with his own. He says something and Jake laughs. Private joke, clearly. They look like a couple who share a lot of private jokes. They

look like a couple.

Jake glances my way, then does a double-take.

"Christ. Not you again."

Adrien's head turns my way. He blinks, his old reveal for processing new information.

"I thought we were done with you." Though Jake doesn't speak loudly, I still get a couple of curious glances from the crowded tables. I smile weakly, feeling as unwelcome as Lt. Columbo popping back for "just one more thing."

I make my way through the maze of tables, chairs and luggage. "Me too. But this won't take long. I just wanted to ask a couple of quick questions. Where are you off to?"

The question is for Adrien, but again it's Jake who answers. "London. An old fashioned traditional English Christmas with the family."

Whose family, I wonder? Lisa has always been rather mysterious about her background. I say cautiously, "That sounds like fun."

"Sure," Jake drawls. "Midnight Mass at St. Paul's, the National Ballet's Nutcracker, pantomimes, Christmas lights in the West End, Christmas carolers in Trafalgar Square, and Christmas Day lunch at someplace called Galvin at Windows. Nonstop fun from morning till night."

No comment from Adrien who downs the rest of his beer in a gulp. Jake watches him and his mouth quirks a little in that way he has.

"You're going to sleep the whole flight, aren't you?"

"If at all possible." Adrien's smile is wry -- and it is all for Jake. The look he turns on me is direct and a little cynical. "Go on. Ask."

"Well..."

"Let's cut to the chase. I already know the big question. Is Jake still doing the clubs?"

Jake looks ceilingward.

"Jeez, there are other questions, you know. Readers like you guys. They hope things are going well for you. They want to know that you're happy and well."

A young and leggy teen with dark hair, blue eyes and a wicked jaw very like Adrien's pauses at their table. "Lisa says we should move to the gate now."

Adrien's expression softens -- as does Jake's watching him. "We'll be there," Adrien assures the girl.

Emma nods and returns to a table tucked against the wall. I spot Lisa, Bill Dauten, and Lauren finishing up lunch.

"So the whole family is headed for London? I don't see Natalie."

"Natalie bailed at the last minute."

"Oh. Did she and Angus ever...?"

Jake grins at Adrien. "Machiavelli here is doing his best to delay the inevitable. He's got Natalie house-sitting and taking care of the dog while Angus shop-sits and takes care of the cat."

"Is that going to work?"

"Maybe not, but at least the dog won't be spending Christmas in a kennel."

"Or the cat," Adrien puts in.

"Right. Ten minutes to blast off," Jake warns me. "You better ask your questions."

"Okay, okay. Have you two moved in together yet? It's been five months since...well, since the shootout on the beach."

Jake looks at Adrien.

"Sort of," Adrien answers. "We've got a house full of boxes, mostly still packed. And people keep shipping us furniture." He throws a quick, exasperated look at the table where Lisa

is offering a forkful of something green to a leery looking Bill Dauten.

"That's the house Lisa used to own? The house in Porter Ranch?"

Adrien nods.

"It's nice furniture," Jake observes. "It's just that it would be nicer if we were picking our own."

"Why aren't you?"

Adrien says, "We are. Well, we plan to. But we've been busy. I was in the middle of renovating the bookstore and Jake was in the middle of selling his house and setting up shop." All at once he looks younger and happier. "He's working out of Cloak and Dagger books now. The other half of the building. In fact, he got a big industrial espionage case two months ago, so that's another thing that's eaten up a lot of

time."

He's smiling at Jake who smiles briefly back before contributing, "And there was the investigation into Argyle's death."

"Oh. How did that go?"

"Argyle left a letter," Jake sounds a little weary.

"That simplified things for everybody Me in

particular."

I can see the concern in Adrien's gaze though all he says is, "It wasn't just the confession. Jake still has a lot of friends on the force. A lot of allies. More than he realizes."

"What he means is, Bill Dauten pulled more strings. More strings than a puppeteer."

Adrien's blue gaze holds Jake's. "Not. True."

"Yeah. Well, I'm just glad it's over and behind us."

I ask, "Is it?"

They both nod, but I can see from the wayAdrien watches Jake that there's some trouble there. Not legal apparently, but something.

Riordan points at Adrien's empty glass. Adrien assents. Riordan leaves the table.

"So you do plan on living together?" I ask as Riordan moves out of earshot -- which is a couple of steps given the noise level of the crowded cafe.

"We're living together now, if you want to get technical. We're both staying at the bookstore till we get the house sorted out."

"How is Jake's family taking it? You two as a couple, I mean."

Adrien's lip curls. "There's a good reason he was afraid his family wouldn't understand. They don't. I don't know that they ever will. I don't know that it's in their emotional makeup to understand, but he spoke to his mom last night. She's trying anyway. I guess that's something."

"Speaking of mothers, how does he get on with Lisa?"

A slow smile curves Adrien's mouth. He laughs.

"That was a truly evil laugh. How about Kate?

Do you ever run into her?"

The laughter is instantly gone. "No. Jake makes sure that we don't run into each other. He cares a lot for her, you know."

They seem to have reached a point of understanding where Jake's caring for Adrien goes without saying.

I change the subject to something neutral and safe. "What was the housewarming gift that Lisa bought you?"

"What housewarming...? Oh. The Grimshaw. Moonlight at Whitby. It's a little painting I saw in a gallery--."

"I remember. Sorry, but we've got a lot of questions to get through. Do you know if the Cross of Rouen was ever recovered?"

"Not that I heard. I think it's decorating some mermaid's living room right now."

I can see Jake making his way back to us, beers in hand. I ask quickly, "What are you getting Jake for Christmas?"

"A year of rent free office space at Cloak and Dagger and a Dick Tracy wrist watch."

"Huh?"

"Jake wouldn't agree to lease a space unless I'd agree to let him pay for it, but if it's a Christmas gift he can't really ob--"

"No. I mean, the Dick Tracy watch."

"Oh. It's an MSN Smart Watch. For when he's on stakeout. It's pretty cool."

As Jake reaches the table, Adrien rises. "Your turn. Back in a sec."

Jake hooks a chair leg with his foot and sits down at the table. He places the full glasses next to the empties. I clear my throat. He shoots me that tawny gaze that makes you want to start babbling where you were on the night in question. His dark eyebrows raise in inquiry.

"Do you ever see Detective Chan?" I start with something safe.

"Sure. He tries to throw the occasional business my way. And he's still part of that writing group that meets at the bookstore."

"How's Adrien's health? He looks a lot better, but I know I won't get an honest answer out of him."

"I think he'd surprise you. He's in excellent health and he's enjoying feeling strong and energetic and planning for the future. That's something he never used to do. Plan for the future."

"He's not overdoing things?"

"He's pretty good about pacing himself. He's a sensible guy."

I've seen Jake with Adrien, and privately I think he must form the supporting pillar of this sensible equation, but all I say is, "That didn't seem to be the opinion of Dr. Shearer."

Jake grimaces. "I don't know what that broad's story was. She put his back up. He doesn't take kindly to being bossed around."

"Ah. Well, that brings me to a rather delicate subject. Is Adrien always--"

"Always?"

"Er, you know. In bed."

His face changes. "That. Every couple has their own dynamic. Adrien is not a submissive personality. I don't know the details of how it was with him and Captain Crunch -- and I don't want to know -- but I'll guarantee you, Adrien didn't always play catcher."

"Does that mean...?"

"It's means we're enjoying exploring all the possibilities between us. That's all. Everything feels new with him. Every day feels new. Every day is new."

"And you don't have any regrets?"

"I have lots of regrets, but I don't regret any choice I've made in the past six months. I don't regret choosing to be with Adrien. That's one thing I'll never regret."

"What about kids?"

Jake's gaze lowers and he picks up his glass.

"There are always tradeoffs. I had this image of a wife and a family all neatly corralled behind a white picket fence, and the fact is, I didn't pick that kind of woman to marry -- and I sure as hell didn't pick that kind of man."

Across the crowded room, the Dautens are on their feet and gathering their belongings. Lisa is shooting worried looks at our table, no doubt wondering where Adrien has got to.

But there he is, coming toward us -- and he does look much healthier and happier than the last time I saw him. Not just healthy and happy. He looks relaxed.

"Darling!" Lisa waves to him.

He raises his hand in acknowledgement and gives Jake a rueful smile.

Jake watches him too, and there's something in his expression I can't quite define. I can't help asking, "Are you going to be able to be faithful to him? Do you still do the clubs?"

Jake shakes his head. "You do the clubs because you can't find what you need at home. I've got everything I need. I've got the answer to needs I didn't even know I had."

From overhead comes the announcement that the flight to London is about to board first class passengers.

"That's us," Adrien mouths to Jake. Jake nods and puts cash down on the table. He pushes back his chair and shrugs into his jacket.

"What did you get him for Christmas?" I ask because I'm out of time and I suddenly can't remember the other questions.

"You mean besides agreeing to keep him company during this holiday in hell?"

"Besides that, yes."

I think for a moment he isn't going to answer. Jake picks up Adrien's jacket and turns away to where Adrien waits for him at the café entrance. Then Jake looks back at me and grins. "For Christmas? Two silk scarves and a white peacock feather."

SO THIS IS CHRISTMAS PLAYLIST

So here we go again. Here's a playlist of the music that inspired the writing of *So This is Christmas.*

Please Come Home for Christmas – The Eagles

God Rest Ye Merry Gentlemen – Sarah McLachlan & Barenaked Ladies

Have Yourself a Merry Little Christmas – Judy Garland

Hallelujah – Rufus Wainwright

The Coldest Night of the Year – She and Him

I've Got My Love to Keep Me Warm – Dean Martin

What are You Doing New Year's Eve – Ella Fitzgerald

My Dear Acquaintance - Peggy Lee

Auld Lang Syne – Celtic Woman

THE
CHRISTMAS
CODAS

THE ADRIEN ENGLISH MYSTERIES

BROKEN HALLELUJAH

Baby, I've been here before
I know this room, I've walked this floor
I used to live alone before I knew you.

Yeah, once upon a time. Halle-fucking-lujah.

The first time he'd heard that song it had been in that very building. Cloak and Dagger Books. It had been around this time of year. Not quite this late in the season. The song was on a Christmas album that Adrien had played a lot. Rufus Wainwright. Jake had never heard of Rufus Wainwright before then. Never heard the song "Hallelujah." Now it seemed to be on every time he turned on the radio.

What the hell did it even mean?

And remember when I moved in you
The holy dove was moving too
And every breath we drew was Hallelujah

Such a weird song. Such a weird time in his life.

It was all over now. Over and done. And he did not believe in wasting time on regrets over the things that could not be changed.

Should not be changed.

But here he sat in his car, watching the dark and silent building across the street.

Sometimes it seemed like a dream, those months. Ten months. Not even a year. How could the most important relationship of his life have been the briefest?

But that's how it felt sometimes. And that's what he would tell Adrien if he had the chance. If Adrien came home alone tonight, Jake would get out of his car, cross the street, and try to tell him…something. It was Christmas Eve after all, and if there was ever a night for holding out an olive branch—for asking forgiveness—this was the night.

That's all he wanted.

That's all he'd ever wanted those other nights he'd parked here. Waiting for the right moment. Trying to get the nerve up.

Maybe there's a God above
But all I've ever learned from love
Was how to shoot at someone who outdrew you

You could refuse to take a phone call, but it was a lot harder to turn away from someone standing in front of you. Too hard for someone as softhearted as Adrien. No, Adrien wouldn't turn him away. Not on Christmas Eve.

But he wasn't coming back tonight.

It was past midnight now. The windows above the bookstore remained dark. The surrounding streets were silent and empty.

Adrien would be at the Dautens'. Or at Snowden's. He'd be with people who loved him. Which was where he belonged. It was where everyone belonged on Christmas Eve.

And Jake…had spent too long sitting here already. He could not afford to arouse suspicion. He did not want to have to lie. Okay, compound the lie. He turned the key in the ignition.

Still, engine idling, exhaust turning red in the taillights, he waited a few minutes longer.

The stars above the city lights twinkled with cheerful indifference, blazing that cold and broken hallelujah.

THE DARK TIDE

A touch so light, so delicate, it was hardly more than a breath, a sigh tracing the length of my throat...bisecting my chest...and then, to my relief, diverging from the roadmap of scars, off-roading to flick the tip of my right nipple.

I arched off the bed. Not far, since my hands were tied to the headboard — tied loosely and with something soft. Silk scarves? I could free myself in an instant, but it wasn't about freedom, was it?

The teasing touch moved to the tip of my other nipple.

I gasped. "That tickles!"

"It's a feather." I could hear the smile in Jake's voice.

"Ah."

The feather ghosted its way over my ribcage...down to my abdomen. I sucked in a breath as the feather dusted and danced still lower...

"How's that feel?"

I nodded. Everything felt lovely, from the cool, crisp linen sheets to Jake's warm breath against my face. The feather teased and thrilled as it brushed across my thigh...groin...thigh...

I wriggled one of my hands free and pulled off the blindfold.

This coda takes place one year after *The Hell You Say*. This is Adrien and Jake's first night in London.

The hotel room was nearly dark in the fading afternoon light. Jake gazed down at me, his mouth quirking. "I wondered how long that would last."

"I like to look at you," I said. "I like to touch you."

He nodded, pulled the other scarf off, freeing my wrist. He lowered himself beside me on the wide four-poster bed, touched the tip of a drooping white peacock feather to my nose. I laughed and blew at the bobbing green-blue eye of the feather.

"How long before your mother's knocking on the door again, do you think?"

"I've got the Do Not Disturb sign out."

"Baby, you're an optimist."

"Maybe." I smiled at him, looped my arm around his neck, pulling him down to me. He kissed me. I kissed him back. "Next year we're staying home for Christmas. I don't care who comes up with what plan."

"Uh huh."

He rested his head on my chest. For a time we lay there, breathing in soft unison, the muted sounds of London traffic providing a soundtrack to our thoughts.

"Regrets?" I asked at last.

Jake raised his head, studying me. He leaned back on his elbow. "No regrets."

I smiled faintly.

He reached out, brushed the hair out of my eyes. "That's not right. I have regrets. I regret the gutless, asinine things I did, the people I hurt. I regret hurting you. I regret the time I wasted. But if all those gutless, asinine things were somehow part of how I got to this moment, then no. I don't regret anything."

Considering what a painful journey he'd had to get to this moment, I thought that was a brave statement.

"You?" Jake asked. "Regrets?"

"Just the time we wasted."

"We're not wasting any more time." He reached around, found the feather.

I could feel my smile turning wry. "Is this going to be enough for you?"

He looked puzzled for an instant. Then his expression grew grave. "This? No. The feather and blindfold routine in an overpriced hotel? No. I need more. I admit it. I need entire nights and entire days. Hundreds of them. Thousands of them. I need breakfast and lunch and dinner and every dessert we can squeeze in. I need every minute we can get."

"For as long as we both shall live?"

"Yeah. That's pretty much it."

I closed my eyes, smiling. "I guess that'll work."

His laugh was quiet. I felt him bend over me, felt his mouth graze mine... My eyes shot open at the soft tap-tap-tapping on our room door.

THE DARK TIDE #2

"**Y**ou were laughing in your sleep last night." Jake's eyes met mine in the mirror over the sink. He was taking his turn shaving in the small hotel bathroom.

"*I* was?"

His cheek creased, and the electric razor accommodated the sudden curves in his still half-bristly face.

"Good to know I'm having a good time," I said.

His brows drew together, and he flicked off the razor. He turned to face me. "*Aren't* you having a good time?"

"Yes!" I don't know who was more surprised at my previous comment. Me or Jake. "Yeah. I'm sure as hell having a better Christmas than the last three years."

"But?" I had his full and thoughtful consideration. Which still caught me off guard sometimes. Jake paid attention to details. No question. Which could occasionally be dismaying when you were used to— and even enjoyed—flying under the radar.

"Are *you* having a good time?" I asked.

"Yes. I am." He said it without hesitation. "We're both here, and we're both healthy. It's our first Christmas together. I've never been happier. That's the truth."

Adrien and Jake's last night in London.

Yes. I could see in his face that it was the truth.

"You don't mind the fact that every minute of this trip is preprogrammed—that our first Christmas is being spent running from one end of London to the next?"

He lifted a negligent shoulder.

"Or that the rare times we're alone, my cell phone rings? Or someone knocks on the door?"

His mouth twitched.

I felt obliged to point out, "We're having our Christmas dinner in a restaurant."

"I've had my Christmas dinner in worse places. I've had years I didn't get a Christmas dinner."

I sighed.

He reached out, unhurriedly pulling me into his arms. He didn't kiss me, though. He studied me, and I studied him. Jake asked, "Are you fretting over the bookstore?"

"No."

"Uh-huh."

I amended, "Well, mostly no. I do hope it's still standing, but I guess we'd have heard if it wasn't. No, mostly I just…wish we were home. I'd have liked our first Christmas to have been a little less busy. Less crowded. We're not even moved in yet. You've got this very small window of free time, and we're using it up here. I guess in a perfect world—"

Jake interrupted quietly, "Let's go home."

"Huh?"

"You've convinced me. Let's leave early. Let's do the Christmas thing with your family this afternoon, and then tomorrow let's see about grabbing an early flight home."

My heart leapt at the idea. But...

I said uncertainly, "I... How can we?"

"Your mother didn't think you'd agree to come at all. She got you here for Christmas. I don't think she's going to kick up too much of a fuss if we check out early."

He was right. Lisa had been as startled as anyone when in a moment of weakness I'd agreed to her plan for a family holiday abroad. I think I'd partly done it because I hoped the change of scenery would help distract Jake from his own family's struggle to accept his coming out. There's nothing like Midnight Mass at St. Paul's to put things into perspective. Provided you don't mind looking at the world through binoculars. Or possibly opera glasses.

Anyway, Christmas in London with all the trimmings had sounded good in theory—and a lot of it had even been good in practice—but the thing I wanted most for Christmas was to...well, it would sound schmaltzy to say it aloud, but through the years there had been a few dreams—no, *dream* was too strong, but there had been some wistful imaginings about spending *this* holiday of all holidays with Jake. Suffice it to say figgy pudding had not played a big role in the proceedings.

But the fact that there even were proceedings...that might explain why I had been laughing in my sleep. *Joy.* It wasn't just for Christmas anymore.

I smiled up at Jake. His heart was thumping steadily against my own. It occurred to me that he was a comfortable place to lean—not that I had ever wanted to lean on anyone, and I didn't plan on making a habit of it, but for these peaceful moments...

"Let's go home," Jake repeated.

I nodded. "Yeah. Okay. Let's go home."

His mouth touched mine. Sweet and warm and tasting a little bit of preshave lotion. I broke the kiss to laugh.

Jake looked surprised.

"Best part of this," I said.

He raised his brows.

"Lisa will totally blame *you*."

THE ADRIEN ENGLISH MYSTERIES

From: *A Coal Miner's Son: Don and Ricky-Joe – A Backwoods Romance*

Ricky-Joe put down his guitar and made a couple of notes. The new song was coming along. Not easily, because a drop of his heart's blood was in every word, but it was coming. And maybe someday Don would hear that song on the radio—or more likely Spotify—and remember…

> *I'd shorely hold up the ceiling of the darkest mine shaft for you*
> *I'm caving in, you cave in too*
> *'Cuz diamonds come from coal, it's true*
> *I'm caving in, you cave in too*

The meter was a little rough. Don had always said timing was Ricky-Joe's problem. But it was no use thinking of Don now. Their second chance at love had gone up in flames with the fire that had destroyed the bonsai orchard. Don would never forgive him, and Ricky-Joe couldn't blame him. Only a fool would leave his guitar in the bright sunlight where a cruel and random sunbeam might glance off those steel strings and spark a raging inferno. You only got so many chances in this bot-

---

Later that same night in London.

tomless mine pit of a world, and Ricky-Joe had wound up with the shaft.

Again.

He wiped a tear away and made another notation on the chord chart.

The door to his motel room burst open, and Don charged in. Ricky-Joe flew to his feet.

"Don!"

Don looked exhausted beneath the grime and coal dust. Actually, it was smudges from the smoke, because it had been a long time since Don had worked the mines. Thank Jiminy Cricket for that, but was it really an improvement if he had to go back to being a butcher's apprentice and killing baby cows? Beneath the weariness in his sapphire eyes was a twinkle.

"Ricky-Joe." Don held up something in his big, strong, workmanlike hand.

Ricky-Joe's eyes popped at the vision of the small and twisted plant. "Donnie, is that what I think it is?"

Don nodded solemnly. "Yonder little fellow survived that conflagration that took out all his leafy kinfolk."

"A baby bonsai," breathed Ricky-Joe.

"Babe, I know you feel to blame for what occurred in the orchard yesterday. I know you must be planning to run away to Nashville again. But this wee limb of greenery is the symbol of our love. A love that can withstand—"

"Something funny?" Jake asked.

"Hm? Oh." I showed him the cover of the paperback. "I found it in the drawer of the bedside table."

His dark brows rose. "*A Coal Miner's Son*? I guess it makes a change from Bibles and phone books."

"You ain't just a-kidding." I smiled at the green plaid flannel pajama bottoms he wore. We hadn't had much time for jammies and such in our previous acquaintanceship. I kind of liked the, well, touch of domesticity official sleepwear brought to the festivities.

However brief their appearance would be.

Jake crawled into bed beside me. His skin looked smooth and supple in the mellow lamplight, his face younger. He smelled of toothpaste and the aftershave he'd worn at dinner.

"I thought that meal would never end," I said. "It felt like we were sitting there for years."

"There did seem like a lot of courses. The food wasn't as bad as I expected, though." Jake glanced at our hotel room clock. "Hey. It's officially Christmas."

"So it is. Happy Christmas."

"Merry Christmas." He nodded at the book I held. "Were you, er, planning to read for much longer?"

I tossed the book to the side. It made a satisfying *thunk* as it hit the wall. "No," I said, and reached for him. "I shorely wasn't."

SO THIS IS CHRISTMAS

Well, baby, I've been here before
I've seen this room, and I've walked this floor
I used to live alone before I knew you
But I've seen your flag on the marble arch
And love is not a victory march
It's a cold and it's a broken Hallelujah

I was humming along with Rufus Wainwright performing Cohen's "Hallelujah" as I ran up the stairs to Jake's office.

"Hey," I said. "I didn't think you were coming back this afternoon."

I stopped in the doorway. Jake stood at the window that overlooked the alley behind the building. I couldn't see his face, but something about the set of his shoulders silenced me. Took my breath away, in fact.

It wasn't defeat exactly. But I got a sense of...weariness that went beyond the physical.

"Jake?"

He tensed, as though he hadn't heard me. As though his mind was a million miles away.

A deleted scene from the novella.

"Yep?"

That glimpse of his eyes froze my heart for a second or two.

He sounded brusque, but that was because…because guys like Jake did not cry. Not when they lost jobs they loved. Not when their marriages broke up. Not when their families wouldn't talk to them.

Maybe he'd cried when Kate lost the baby. He'd never said.

I'd never ask.

He was not crying. His eyes were a little red. It could even be allergies. He probably was genuinely…weary.

Or it could be the result of meeting Kate today. Of course he would feel regret. Wish he'd made different choices. Maybe he was comparing the might-have-beens against the what-he-was-left-withs.

"Everything okay?" I could hear the mix of wariness and worry in my voice.

His smile was twisted, but some of the bleakness in his eyes faded. "Yes."

"You're sure?"

He walked toward me, still smiling that crooked smile. I didn't realize I had left the doorway until I met him halfway.

I slid my arms around his neck; he wrapped his arms around my waist.

He said softly, "I'm very sure."

ABOUT THE AUTHOR

Bestselling author of over sixty titles of classic Male/Male fiction featuring twisty mystery, kickass adventure, and unapologetic man-on-man romance, **JOSH LANYON** has been called "arguably the single most influential voice in m/m romance today."

Her work has been translated into nine languages. The FBI thriller *Fair Game* was the first Male/Male title to be published by Harlequin Mondadori, the largest romance publisher in Italy. The Adrien English series was awarded the All Time Favorite Couple by the Goodreads M/M Romance Group. Josh is an Eppie Award winner, a four-time Lambda Literary Award finalist (twice for Gay Mystery), and the first ever recipient of the Goodreads All Time Favorite M/M Author award.

Josh is married and lives in Southern California.

Find other Josh Lanyon titles at www.joshlanyon.com

Follow Josh on *Twitter*, *Facebook*, and *Goodreads*.

ALSO BY JOSH LANYON

NOVELS

The ADRIEN ENGLISH Mysteries

Fatal Shadows • *A Dangerous Thing* • *The Hell You Say*

Death of a Pirate King • *The Dark Tide*

Stranger Things Have Happened • *So This is Christmas*

The HOLMES & MORIARITY Mysteries

Somebody Killed His Editor • *All She Wrote*

The Boy with the Painful Tattoo

The ALL'S FAIR Series

Fair Game • *Fair Play* • *Fair Chance (coming soon)*

The A SHOT IN THE DARK Series

This Rough Magic

The ART OF MURDER Series

The Mermaid Murders

OTHER NOVELS

The Ghost Wore Yellow Socks • *Mexican Heat (with Laura Baumbach)*

Strange Fortune • *Come Unto These Yellow Sands* • *Stranger on the Shore*

Winter Kill • *Jefferson Blythe, Esquire* • *Murder in Pastel*

The Curse of the Blue Scarab

NOVELLAS

The DANGEROUS GROUND Series

Dangerous Ground • Old Poison • Blood Heat
Dead Run • Kick Start

The I SPY Series

I Spy Something Bloody • I Spy Something Wicked
I Spy Something Christmas

The IN A DARK WOOD Series

In a Dark Wood • The Parting Glass

The DARK HORSE Series

The Dark Horse • The White Knight

The DOYLE & SPAIN Series

Snowball in Hell

The HAUNTED HEART Series

Haunted Heart Winter

The XOXO FILES Series

Mummie Dearest

OTHER NOVELLAS

Cards on the Table • *The Dark Farewell* • *The Darkling Thrush*
The Dickens with Love • *Don't Look Back* • *A Ghost of a Chance*
Lovers and Other Strangers • *Out of the Blue* • *A Vintage Affair*
Lone Star (in Men Under the Mistletoe)
Green Glass Beads (in Irregulars) • *Everything I Know*
Blood Red Butterfly • *Baby, It's Cold (in Comfort and Joy)*
A Case of Christmas • *Murder Between the Pages*

SHORT STORIES

A Limited Engagement • *The French Have a Word for It*
In Sunshine or In Shadow • *Until We Meet Once More*
Icecapade (in His for the Holidays) • *Perfect Day* • *Heart Trouble*
In Plain Sight • *Wedding Favors* • *Wizard's Moon*
Fade to Black • *Night Watch*

COLLECTIONS

The SWEET SPOT Collection: PETIT MORTS

Other People's Weddings • *Slings and Arrows*
Sort of Stranger Than Fiction • *Critic's Choice* • *Just Desserts*
Merry Christmas, Darling (Holiday Codas)